DARK LIFE

KAT FALLS

SCHOLASTIC INC.
New York Toronto London Auckland
Sydney Mexico City New Delhi Hong Kong

For Declan, Vivienne, and Connor, who inspire me to go for the funny and the "cool!" And Bob, the love of my life.

This book was originally published in hardcover by Scholastic Press in 2010.

ISBN 978-0-545-17815-0

15 14 13 15 16/0

Printed in the U.S.A. 40

First paperback printing, February 2011

CHAPTER

ONE

I peered into the deep-sea canyon, hoping to spot a toppled skyscraper. Maybe even the Statue of Liberty. But there was no sign of the old East Coast, just a sheer drop into darkness.

A ball of light shot past me—a vampire squid, trailing neon blue. The glowing cloud swirled around my helmet. Careful not to break it up, I drifted onto my knees, mesmerized. But my trance was cut short by a series of green sparks bursting out of the gorge. I fell back, every muscle in my body tense. Only one fish glittered like an emerald and traveled in a pack: the green lantern shark. Twelve inches long and deadly as piranhas, they could rip apart something twenty times their size. Forget what they could do to a human.

I should have seen them coming, even this deep. I should have known the squid had squirted its radiant goo to divert a predator. And now my helmet's crown lights served as an even brighter beacon. With a jab to my wrist screen, I snapped them off, but it was too late—I couldn't unring that dinner bell.

I pried a flare gun from my belt and fired into the midst of the electric green frenzy. Two heartbeats later, light exploded over the canyon, shocking the sharks into stillness, eyes and teeth glittering. Quickly, I scooped the anchor of my mantaboard out of the muck and hauled myself onto it. Lying on my stomach with my legs dangling, I twisted the handgrips and took off, making serious wake. If my lungs hadn't been filled with Liquigen, I would've whooped aloud.

Not that I was in the clear. As soon as the flare died, the sharks would be on me like suckerfish on a whale. I thought about burying myself in the thick ooze of the seafloor. Bedding down with the boulder-sized clams had worked before. I chanced a look over my shoulder. Sure enough, the darkness twinkled with stars—vicious little stars, shooting my way.

Tilting the manta into a nosedive, I flicked on the head beams, only to have the light reflect off metal. A sub! I crashed into it and toppled, boots over helmet. The manta's handgrips tore from my fingers as I slammed onto my back. Sliding down the sloped hull, I grappled for a hold without luck until my feet hit the bumper and I stopped short. My guts took longer to settle.

Without a rider, the manta would shut off automatically; I'd have to find it later. Right now, I needed to take cover. But why was this little rig sitting on the seafloor without a light on to announce its presence? Was it a wreck? If so, it hadn't sunk that long ago. The polished metal hull was barnacle free.

I scuttled along the bumper until I found the circular door to the air lock. The panel cover dangled from one hinge with pry marks scoring its edge. I hesitated, wondering about those marks, when suddenly the hull gleamed with emerald light.

I slammed the entry button. Like a dilating eye, the hatch opened and seawater filled the small chamber. Plunging into the air lock, I whirled to see sharks streaking toward me from all sides. I hit the interior button whole-handed. As the hatch clinched shut, the sharks plowed into it like mini torpedoes. From inside, they sounded like Death pounding at the door. I slumped against the chamber wall and grinned. Nothing put a buzz in my blood like escaping predators.

How many rules had I just broken? Visiting Coldsleep Canyon alone: forbidden. On nothing but a mantaboard: absolutely forbidden. Exploring a derelict sub: off the sonar screen. But now I had to take cover until the sharks left. It was the smart thing to do. The safe thing. Not that my parents would ever hear about the sub or the sharks. With a gang of outlaws roaming the territory, they had enough to worry about.

When the last drop of seawater disappeared through the grated floor, I tipped back my helmet and inhaled. The air was rank but did its job: The oxygen-infused liquid in my lungs evaporated. Switching on my flash-light, I opened the next hatch and stepped right into someone else's nightmare.

Blood dripped from every surface in the gear room—walls, benches, lockers. . . . Wet and glistening, it puddled around the prospecting tools that littered the floor. I slowed my breath as if that would lessen the metallic tang that now filled my nose—a stink that conjured up the blood-slicked deck of a whaling ship. *Some fisherman butchered something big in here, that's all,* I told myself. A sunfish or a marlin. Nothing to panic about. Except . . . I edged farther into the room. No matter how hard it thrashed, a dying fish couldn't have emptied the weapons rack, let alone ripped it off the wall.

Circling the overturned rack, I panned my light across the open lockers—all ransacked—and tugged at my suit's neck ring. Usually my helmet didn't bother me when it hung off the back of my diveskin, but now its weight choked me. The sharks outside weren't doing my nerves any favors, either, knocking along the sub's hull, looking for a way in.

As soon as the sharks stopped tapping, I'd head up to the sunlight zone and hunt for dinner like I should have been doing all along. But the tapping didn't stop. If anything, it grew louder. Worse, I realized it wasn't the sharks tapping at all, but . . .

Footsteps.

I snapped off my flashlight and let the darkness envelop me. The sub might be eerie and blood splattered, but that was no ghost tromping down the hall. Silently, I peeled off my gloves and drew my speargun from the holster on my back.

Ghosts weren't real. But outlaws were.

For months, the Seablite Gang had terrorized the settlement, robbing every supply ship that floated our way. I had often wondered what would happen if I came across them.

Now it looked like I was getting my chance.

I hoisted the speargun over my shoulder, only to have the cold metal slip through my fingers. Grabbing at air, I snagged the strap just before the gun clattered to the floor. In the corridor, the footsteps broke into a trot.

I crouched behind a crate and took aim at the door. As the footsteps neared, I curled my finger around the trigger. I tried to steady my breathing but couldn't steady my arm. It was one thing to shoot a hungry tiger shark, but skewering a person—even a low-down outlaw—I didn't know if I had the stomach for it. Suddenly, a flashlight beam shot into the room and whipped across my face, blinding me. I lifted my speargun and a scream rang out—not mine—and the light went out. I scrambled to my feet and sprinted into the corridor, following the echoing footsteps into the sub's bridge.

That scream—it hadn't been an outlaw.

It had been a girl.

"I won't hurt you!" I called out.

No reply.

"Look." I aimed the flashlight at my speargun while holstering it. "Don't be afraid."

Like the gear room, the bridge was a mess. No pools of blood, thankfully. But the equipment consoles had been stripped and wires sprouted from the ceiling. One bunch swayed like seaweed, telling me someone had just passed. As I parted the wires, a light snapped on and a high-pitched voice demanded, "Who are you?"

Surprised, I turned my flashlight toward the voice. But my reply evaporated as a girl strode toward me, her long, dark braid swishing.

"You scared me!" she said. In one fist she gripped a flashlight, and in the other, a green knife. Her hold on both was shaky, yet defiance blazed in her pale blue eyes.

"Sorry," I managed to say, despite my shock. She looked about my age, fifteen. But more astounding, she was from Above. No doubt about it. Between her pink cheeks and peeling nose, her face was a study in UV exposure.

She stumbled to a halt. "Are you a ghost?"

Inside, I went very still. Just once, I would've liked to meet a Topsider who didn't make me feel like a freak. I never said anything about their sunburns.

She squared her shoulders as if bracing for the worst. "You are, aren't you?"

I almost nodded to see what she'd do. But instead I said, "I'm alive and human. Just like you."

"You're glowing," she accused.

For light's sake, so my skin shimmered. That didn't make me a ghost. I wasn't skeletal or hollow eyed. I'd built up lean muscle from working on the homestead, and my eyes were a perfectly normal shade of kelp green. "I'm not *glowing*," I told her. "It's called a shine." I tried not to sound defensive. "It comes from eating bioluminescent fish."

The girl inched closer. "People don't eat fish that glow in the dark."

"Down here we do."

"Really? That's so—" Bounding forward, she jabbed me in the ribs with her flashlight. I gasped in pain while she gasped even louder. "Hot tar! You are real."

A reply, even a sarcastic one, was beyond me. Not only had she knocked the breath from my lungs, I couldn't believe she'd thought her flashlight would go right through me. Heck, I was lucky she hadn't tested my humanness with her knife.

"I thought," she stammered, "I mean, in the dark you—"

"I don't glow."

"No," she agreed too quickly, holstering her green knife. "Of course you don't. I'm very sorry. Are you all right?" She moved in close again, pushing her long bangs out of her eyes.

"I'll live." Though by tomorrow I'd have a bruise the size of a mud-eating sea cucumber.

"Did you see all the blood when you came in?" she asked.

"Fish blood, probably." At least I hoped so. Like most Topsiders, she stood too close. I could feel her sucking up the oxygen around me and it was making me lightheaded. I edged back. "What are you doing here?"

"I came aboard hoping this was my brother's sub. Now I'm hoping it's not. . . ." She waved her flashlight across the ransacked consoles. "He's down here somewhere, panning for manganese nodules."

"Black pearls. That's what we call them—well, prospectors do. Like your brother. Wait, are you saying you're alone?"

"You're alone." She said it like she'd proven something.

"I live down here. I was the first person ever born subsea. You're a—" Did Topsiders mind being called Topsiders? I didn't know, but I sure hated it when they called the pioneers Dark Life.

"A what? I'm a what?"

"From Above," I amended.

"Above." She smiled as if the word amused her. "As in 'above the water'?"

"Yeah."

"How do you know?"

"How do I know . . . ?"

"That I'm from *Above*?"

Was she serious? Even if she hadn't commented on my shine, everything about her hollered "Topsider." Worse, she had all the telltale signs of an amateur diver. But aloud, I just said, "Freckles." At her puzzled look, I added, "Kids down here don't have them." Her whole face looked as if it had been sprinkled with wet sand. I aimed my flashlight higher. "Then there's your hair."

"My hair?" She didn't sound so amused anymore.

"It's streaky."

Her hair, which was brown like mine, had stripes of copper running through it. Why did the sun lighten people's hair but darken their skin? I didn't get that.

"Streaky . . ." She flipped her long braid over her shoulder, out of my sight.

I thrust out my hand. "I'm Ty."

She hesitated before taking it and, of course, didn't tug off her dive glove. Among settlers, it would've been an insult. But then, Topsiders rarely showed skin except from the neck up. Sometimes not even that.

"I'm Gemma."

"Gemma." I couldn't help smiling. "Like *gem o' the ocean*."

She looked startled. "What's that from?"

"It's what we say down here when we come across something pretty." I realized it sounded like I was saying that she was pretty, which I wasn't—even though she was. My mouth went dry. "You know, like a shell." I cleared my throat. "Or a sea slug."

"Sea slugs are pretty?" she asked skeptically.

"They can be."

"That's how my brother began his last letter." She ran her fingers over the pocket where she'd stowed her knife. "'To Gem o' the ocean.'"

"Well, if he lives down here, he'd know the expression."

"Look—I lost my minisub," she said abruptly and tipped up her chin, daring me to laugh at her.

I wasn't even tempted. "Where'd you get a minisub?"

"At the Trade Station. I rented it from an old card player." She plucked at her baggy diveskin. "Now I'll have to pay him for it."

The guy had to be a professional gambler. The Trade Station was crawling with them. "Did you rent that diveskin from him, too? Because it doesn't fit right." Just looking at the way the metallic fabric hung limply around her slim waist was enough to make me break a sweat.

The sensors were woven between the layers of material. If the diveskin wasn't hugging her body, its computer wasn't getting an accurate read on her vitals.

With an impatient flick of her hand, she dismissed my worry. "I left my sub by the air lock. But now, it's—what?"

"You really came down here alone?" I just couldn't wrap my brain around that. Even scientists who were experts on the deep sea brought crews and lots of equipment.

"Let me guess, you think girls should wear long dresses and 'practice obedience' in order to stop the Rising."

"No," I replied carefully, though I guessed from her tone that she didn't hold with the New Puritan belief that global warming was God's way of punishing us for our sins. "It's just that it's really dangerous subsea."

"I could get eaten by a giant squid—I know." She rolled her eyes. "I was in the water for two seconds."

"If a squid wants to eat you, it doesn't have to wait for you to get wet." That got her attention. "A giant squid can come eighty feet long and weigh a ton. It'll drag your vehicle so deep, the water pressure will crack it into pieces. Then that squid will pluck you out like it's shucking a clam."

Under her freckles, she paled. "You're trying to scare me."

"Yeah," I admitted. "But that doesn't mean I'm lying." She shouldn't be deep diving without knowing the risks. Though I had to give her credit for sheer guts.

"Why would anyone want to live down here?" she asked with a shudder.

"Does your family own any land?"

"Of course not. There isn't enough to go around."

"My family owns two hundred acres."

She wrinkled her nose. "At the bottom of the sea."

"Yeah. But it's ours." If she saw my family's homestead—saw how green and beautiful it was—maybe then she'd understand. "When I'm eighteen, I'm going to stake my own claim. A hundred acres between two buttes."

"You sound like an ad for the Subsea Homestead Act." Smiling, she quoted the commercial: "*'Stake your claim, work the land for five years, and it's yours!'* Wait—what's that sound?"

A shrill clicking vibrated through the hull. Our eyes darted to the ceiling and then to the inky water outside the viewing dome. Growing louder and faster, the clicking turned into a piercing trill, then something crashed into the curved window. With a shriek, Gemma threw her arms over her head but the flexiglass didn't shatter. Instead a dark object bumped down the window, trailing a thick chain.

"Tow hook." I shut off my flashlight and pushed past her to peer up through the dome. "Kill your light." High above us, a sub hovered with its exterior lights glowing softly, outlining its shape—a shape I'd heard described many times, always in fearful tones. The heavy hook hit the rig's bumper with a thud that reverberated through the soles of my boots and up my spine. I backed away. "Let's get out of here."

A path of light shot down through the darkness. "Come on," I urged, but Gemma's gaze stayed on the chain outside, now taut and writhing in the spotlight's beam. "That's the *Specter* up there," I tried to explain. "It belongs to—" A pair of boots thunked onto the viewing dome and kicked off again. Then the rest of the man shimmied into view. When he let go of the chain and dropped onto the bumper, a second man slid down after him.

Now Gemma skittered back into the shadows. "Who are they?"

I crouched as thin beams of light crisscrossed the bridge, coming from the men's helmets. "Outlaws," I whispered, tugging her down.

"Really?"

She looked outside with new interest as the outlaws attached the tow hook to the rig. With every move they made, their crown lights bounced wildly inside the bridge.

I touched my thigh where I had seven inches of serrated steel holstered. Still, as skilled as I was with a knife and speargun, I knew I couldn't fend off a sub full of grown men. We had to get out of this rig unnoticed. I nudged Gemma and pointed at the corridor. After a last look at the outlaws, she followed me into the dark hall. At the gear room, I flicked on my flashlight and stepped through the hatchway.

She didn't budge from the threshold. "Does this mean it's not fish blood?"

"I don't know," I admitted. Until now, there had been no proof that the Seablite Gang had ever killed anyone, only a heap of ugly stories and a bullet in a skipper's leg—enough to convince me that I didn't want to tangle with an outlaw. Around us, the hull moaned and creaked. "Hurry." I circled the room to avoid the blood. "Once they haul this wreck out of the mud, it'll fly."

"I'm not going outside." She hovered in the corridor. "I'll hide somewhere in here."

Maybe I shouldn't have told her about the giant squids. "Listen," I said, "if the Seablite Gang killed someone in here"— with a shudder, the sub lurched forward, and I grabbed on to the air lock's hatch frame to keep from falling over — "you can bet they're dumping this rig right into Coldsleep Canyon. You want to go down with it?"

Blanching, she dashed into the air lock. "Tell me again why people live down here," she said.

I hit the button that closed the hatch behind her. "When you suck it in, do it all the way."

She flushed anemone pink. "Excuse me?"

"The Liquigen." Flipping her helmet over her head, I snapped its seal shut. "Some beginners leave pockets of air in their lungs. Then, when they get into the black, their chests are smashed flat by the water pressure." I clapped my hands together for effect.

The icy glare she shot me could have restored the glaciers. But my words must have sunk in, because she bit down on the Liquigen tube in the base of her helmet and made an effort to fill her lungs. As she gagged and snorted, she fell against the chamber wall, setting off a blinking red light above the exterior hatch. I secured my own helmet, only to realize with a jolt that Gemma couldn't have set off the light. That light only pulsed when someone *outside* pushed the entry button.

I snapped off my flashlight—and not a second too soon. The hatch dialed open and a stream of water shot into the air lock, glistening like a blood spurt in the pulsing red light. The stream widened into a waterfall and churning water climbed over our bodies. I unspooled a short length of rip cord from my belt, clipped the end to Gemma's belt, and steered her to the wall near the open hatch.

As soon as the ocean filled the chamber, a beam of light cut through the bubbles. A helmet light. I waited, nerves firing, as a dark figure stepped through the hatch. The instant he crossed the chamber, I darted outside, dragging Gemma with me. Given our speed, he must have felt the water ripple behind him. He wheeled around, looking younger than I'd expected. Or maybe he just seemed it with his mouth hanging open and black eyes wide at seeing the two of us. In a burst of movement, he slashed forward, baring teeth that had been filed into points and bleached till they were as transparent as a dragonfish's fangs.

Thrusting Gemma behind me, I slammed the entry button. As the hatch cinched shut, the outlaw threw out a hand, grabbing for my neck. The metal plates closed around his forearm. His fingers raked my chest, not trying to snag me anymore but convulsing under the pressure. Stumbling back, I banged into Gemma and knocked her off the bumper into the gloom. The rip cord between us snapped taut and then yanked me into the darkness after her.

For an instant, I sprawled in the ooze, my legs entwined with hers, then I barrel rolled away from the rig, taking Gemma with me. A second later the sub lifted off the seafloor, kicking up silt as it went, sailing into the darkness.

I got to my feet, only to tumble back into the mud when Gemma grabbed on to my dive belt. Did she think I was going to leave her? The rip cord still linked us. As we got up together, she gripped my hand like a moray eel chomping prey. I supposed the freezing darkness and intense pressure could be nerve-wracking if you weren't used to it, which was why the other settlers almost never left the continental shelf. They didn't share my fascination with Coldsleep Canyon, even though it was longer and deeper than the Grand Canyon and a hundred times creepier. Coldsleep had been named the Hudson Canyon until a chunk of the East Coast slid into its gaping maw. Now everyone associated the chasm with death and destruction. I just associated it with predators.

I checked around us for the green lantern sharks. Seeing none, I turned my crown lights on dim and located my mantaboard. Gemma matched me step for step with her lights blazing and knife out. The glare would attract every beast in the area and her knife wouldn't stop half of them, but if waving it around made her feel better, great.

Luckily, her needle-nosed vehicle was whirling in a brine pool only two hundred yards away. A wealthy Topsider's toy. A real beauty. I held the anchor chain taut so she could shimmy up to the gel-filled ring that was the entry port. I followed, pausing to hitch my manta to the jet's tail, where it hovered, resembling a real manta ray, minus the tail. I wiggled inside and spilled onto the pilot bench alongside her. It was like settling into a small, perfect rocket.

After unsealing my helmet, I drew in a breath to make the Liquigen in my lungs evaporate. Because we'd filled our lungs with liquid and not some volatile mix of gasses, our chances of getting the bends were slim. Still, I was glad to see that Gemma had turned on the vehicle's depressurization system. Beside me, she coughed up Liquigen. "Don't hack it out," I instructed, stowing our helmets behind the seat. "That's harder on your lungs."

She swallowed, eyes watering.

"You know this isn't really a minisub, right?" My fingers whispered over the control panel. "It's a jet-fin. Not made for deep diving." As I touched the icon that turned the toggle switches on the panel into holograms, I realized she was staring at me. "Sorry. You want to drive? It's your rental."

"No." Her voice was shaky. "I'm sure you've been piloting subs since you were five."

"Four," I said with a smile she didn't return. "Want me to take you back to the Trade Station?" She nodded, her eyes shining with a mix of alarm and fascination—the way my little sister gazed at mammals with fur. "I have to go anyway to report that rig." To avoid her stare, I searched for the switch that would draw up the anchor. Nothing good ever followed that kind of look.

"How did you find my sub in the dark?" she asked.

"Your jet-fin. Minisubs aren't tricked out for speed."

"You didn't answer the question."

I shrugged, though my insides whirled like a comb jelly. I'd spooked her. And here I thought I was acting normal.

"I just followed the current," I said. Which was true. Sort of. "Any pioneer could do it." I jimmied the throttle and the jet-fin blasted forward, throwing us back against the seat. I knew Gemma was still watching me; I could feel it. I tried to focus on the thrill of the ride, but even that didn't unclench my gut.

"It's true, isn't it?" Soft and insistent, her words poked at me. "What they say about the pioneer kids down here."

"They say a lot of things, but it's all chum." I kept my eyes on the viewport and increased the jet's speed. "We're just like you."

"No, you're not."

She may as well have jabbed me with her flashlight again. In fact, I would have preferred it. Bruises went away. I turned to defend myself, but Gemma's gaze was as bright and intense as the flare I'd fired at the green lantern sharks. And like those deep-sea creatures, I froze.

"Admit it," she said. "You have a Dark Gift."

CHAPTER
TWO

My expression was calm. "Dark Gifts are a myth." I listened to my own voice. Distant. Almost bored. Good. I returned my gaze to the glowing blue control panel and added, "So's the kraken, by the way."

"You found my sub, my jet-fin, in water blacker than tar," she pointed out. "You swam right to it."

"If you think I can see in the dark—I can't. I just followed the river."

"A river in the ocean?" she scoffed. "That makes no sense."

I forced the pedal to the floor to keep from shaking my head in disgust. There was so much she didn't know about the deep sea, yet here she was, paddling around two miles from the ocean's surface. "And you all call *us* crazy," I muttered.

"Who does?"

"You." I yanked the joystick toward me, sending the jet-fin zooming up the continental slope. "Topsiders."

"Topsiders?" She didn't sound offended. "You mean

people who live . . ." Grinning, she waved over her head. "Above."

"Yeah."

Her hand dropped. "You changed the subject."

"Because there are plenty of real things to worry about in the ocean, without fixating on some old fisherman's tale."

"Okay, fine." She made a big show of fastening her seat belt. "Maybe you don't have a Dark Gift. But they are real."

"As real as mermaids."

We traveled the next fifteen minutes in silence while outside the ocean was a blur of blue. With her lips pursed, Gemma stared out the viewport.

There had always been tension between Topsiders and pioneers. After everything we'd been through—the floods, the subsea landslide that sliced through our telecommunications cables and cut us off from the world, and fifty-two years of living under Emergency Law—you would think that we would've gotten along. But that wasn't how it worked. The Topsiders clung to the chunks of oversea land that were still left, and they didn't understand why we weren't clinging, too. For them, it was natural to crowd hundreds of thousands of people into a single square mile. But to live underwater? *That* was unnatural. Though honestly, the people who live on the small ocean townships aren't given much more in the way of respect. Never mind that it is the ocean dwellers who supply the nation's food and keep watch over the energy sources—the tides and hydrothermal vents. We were still freaks to them.

Gemma must have been thinking along the same lines, although from her side of the equation. She turned to me abruptly and said, "There's a boy who lives down here—he talks to dolphins."

I held in my sigh. "We all talk to dolphins. They're like dogs."

"I mean he understands them." Schools of fish surrounded us now that we were on the continental shelf, yet Gemma kept her blue gaze pinned to me. "His name is Akai. A doctor wrote about him in a medical journal."

"You read medical journals?"

"No, but it was reposted all over the newsweb. The doctor thinks Akai's brain developed differently because of the water pressure down here."

I rolled my eyes but she went on.

"Adults aren't affected. Their brains are already formed. Only kids get Dark Gifts."

"Good theory." With a jerk of the joystick, I leveled off the jet-fin. "Must be why people still believe it even though that article was proved to be a big hoax. Guess that wasn't reposted all over the newsweb."

"You *do* know about Akai." Her expression was triumphant.

"What I know is that such crackpot theories are ruining Benthic Territory." I couldn't stifle my anger. "Folks are scared to settle down here because they think their kids will turn into mutants."

"I think it would be cool to have a Dark Gift."

"Your parents wouldn't. They'd worry about your messed-up brain."

"My parents are dead."

I twitched with surprise. She'd said it right out. Like it didn't matter.

"I'm sorry," I said.

"I'm a ward of the Commonwealth. It's no big deal."

I gave her a look, telling her that I wasn't buying it.

"How about this? You believe me when I say I'm fine, and I'll believe you when you say you don't have a Dark Gift." An enormous glowing ball appeared in the murky water ahead of us. An island of light in the cobalt sea. "What is that?"

"The Trade Station," I replied, surprised. "You rented the jet-fin there."

"No, I was on top of the water. On a big floating ring with lots of people."

"That's just the Surface Deck. An elevator takes you down to the lower station. See the cable?" The Trade Station was tethered one hundred feet below the ocean's surface. A thick cable connected it to the floating platform above while anchor chains, studded with tiny lights, dropped into the darkness below.

"Want to know what I do like about the Topside?" I tried for a light tone.

She nodded.

"Getting there!"

CHAPTER

THREE

The jet-fin rocketed out of the ocean and into the otherworldly realm of air and sun. As it arced twenty feet over the ocean's surface, Gemma screamed with delight and clapped when we splashed down in a whirlwind of spray. "Glacial!"

Shielding my eyes, I flipped the motor into idle and let the jet-fin rock with the swells. Sunlight flooded my irises—too hot, too bright.

"Hey, are you okay?" As she bent to see my face, her braid brushed my wrist, sending a shiver through me.

"I'm fine." I wasn't. But I would be able to fake it in a minute. Forcing my hand down, I squinted at the endless expanse of ocean surrounding us. As always, surfacing threw my senses into shock. Overbright colors and sharp-edged sounds assaulted me. How was anyone comfortable up here? The light alone kicked every thought out of my mind and swapped my personality for a headache.

I slid back the cockpit cover, wincing as heat rolled over me. The weird thing about natural air was that unlike filtered air, it had taste—flavored by whatever was nearby. In this case, the sun and ocean—hot and briny. I inhaled and gauged our distance from the floating Surface Deck. From here, the four-story elevator shaft topped with a white glass observatory looked like a mast and full-blown sail. But even as far off as we were, the din of voices carried across the water. I hated market days. To top it off, I hadn't come equipped to surface. Didn't have a hat or even sun-goggles to shield me. Not just from the deadly UV rays, like most people, but the stares.

I stood up in my seat. "I'll meet you at the docking-ring."

"Where are you—" Gemma's words cut out as I dove under the water, back into the sea's cool embrace. Instantly, my mood improved. With two kicks, I was behind the jet-fin, where I unclipped the mantaboard's towline.

"Race you!" I called to Gemma, who was leaning over the other side of the jet. She whirled around as I pulled myself onto the manta. With a twist to its handgrips, the board shot across the waves like a skipping stone.

"You didn't say go!" she shouted. Behind me, the jet-fin roared to life, then sliced past with Gemma waving from the open cockpit.

I rose to my feet and toed the joystick to high and the manta sprang forward, while wind and sea spray slapped my face. I'd say this much for the Topside: Everything moved faster up here, without tons of water weighing it down.

As I approached the Surface Deck, the noise went into attack mode. Hollering vendors, haggling shoppers, and screeching gulls. I slowed the manta until I risked sinking it and focused on the brightly colored stalls that circled the promenade. Even more calming was the sight of the boats clustered along the docking-ring at water level. At least most of the people on the Surface Deck wore tunics with loose-fitting pants, which meant they were probably floaters—people who lived on houseboats. Even if they hadn't seen a shine firsthand, most would know what it was and so would the fishermen. Hopefully.

I almost never came up here. I'd learned long ago that it wasn't a place for me. And I'd learned that the hard way.

There was no turning back now, though. Not with Gemma leading me forward. I rounded a barge and spotted the *Seacoach* in the next slip, unfolding its wing-sails like an enormous albino bat about to take flight. My unease evaporated when I saw my neighbor Jibby Groot on the deck, hosing down the solar membranes that stretched between the wings' struts to catch sunlight and wind. Cruising between the moored boats, I called, "Need a tow?"

Jibby raised his shaggy blond head and, upon spotting me, cracked a gap-toothed smile. "Just the glow stick I want to see."

"I don't glow." I sliced my board into a wave while cutting the motor, which sent a sheet of seawater crashing over him. Laughter and applause erupted nearby and I saw several other young men—all newbie settlers like Jibby—lounging by the ship's deckhouse. As I returned their waves, Jibby jumped onto the docking-ring.

"Where're you headed?" I asked, grasping his outstretched hand.

He hauled me onto the docking-ring, mantaboard and all. "Paramus," he said. "The station is out of everything, thanks to the chum-sucking outlaws. We're going to see what we can scrounge. Want to come?"

"Can't." I folded in the manta's wings to make it easier to carry. "I've got to see the ranger."

"Good luck. He's below—in the town meeting."

"Why aren't you?" I asked with surprise. I'd been itching to hear what was to be "an announcement of vital importance, concerning all territory residents" (according to the sign posted in the Trade Station). But my parents were under the illusion that chores took priority.

"If I wanted to sit indoors and jaw," Jibby retorted, "I'd still be living in a stack-city." A sly grin pulled at his lips. "Ranger Grimes will be in that meeting for hours.

Your parents, too. Come on. We'll hitch your manta to the back and do some wakeboarding."

"Tempting. But I still can't. I'm helping someone." No way was I going to mention Gemma to Jibby, who was on the lookout for a bride. Last year, he'd tried to order one but demanded a refund when she'd arrived, older than his granny.

"Someone?" he asked, interest piqued.

"Ty!" Down the bustling docking-ring, Gemma waved at me with both arms. So much for keeping her stowed away. She'd parked herself between an orange ladder that led up to the promenade and a door to the lounge, which was a fancy name for the hollow space furnished with lockers and benches inside the Surface Deck. Fishermen clustered around her, each bare-chested and slathered in a different color of zinc-paste—orange, green, blue—to protect their skin from the sun.

Whistling soft appreciation, Jibby patted down his damp hair and strode toward her. So debonair. Having no better choice, I swung my mantaboard over my shoulder and followed him. We reached Gemma just as the fishermen dispersed. The last one handed her back a laminated photograph, saying, "Don't recognize him."

"It's a really old picture," she called after the man. "Imagine him grown-up."

"Howdy," Jibby crooned, closing in.

She glanced over her shoulder, as if he was talking to someone else, which irritated me. She knew that he was slobbering over her and not any of the sweaty, color-streaked fishermen pushing past. True, some were women, but who could tell the difference when they were coated up to their eyeballs in a mixture of zinc-paste, grime, and stray fish scales?

Reluctantly, I introduced Gemma to Jibby.

"So"—Jibby shot me a smirk—"you're *someone*."

"I hope so," Gemma replied. "Usually I'm just one of a million someones."

"Welcome to Benthic Territory, Gemma." Jibby thrust out his hand. "Where you're not only someone, you're a rarity."

Her brow puckered as if she didn't know what to say. Looking away, I inhaled the ocean's briny scent to ease the ache behind my eyes. She hadn't acted flustered with me. No, she'd jabbed me with a flashlight and wouldn't let up about Dark Gifts.

I heard her ask, "Have you seen him around here?" and glanced back to see her thrust the photo into Jibby's outstretched hand. Suddenly my head felt much better.

"That your brother?" I asked.

She nodded. "So far, no one recognizes him. But he's only fourteen in the picture. I don't have anything recent."

"Sorry." Jibby handed her back the photo. "Haven't seen him."

"His name is Richard." She rubbed her thumb across the image, as if to brush her brother's long hair out of his eyes. "Richard Straid."

"You look a lot like him," Jibby said.

I frowned at him over her bent head. The resemblance between the siblings was slight at best. Both had blue eyes and reddish-brown hair, but Gemma's brother was a tall, fishing rod of a boy with features too big for his face. Still, she brightened at the comparison.

"Don't bother showing his photo to fishermen," I advised. "Prospectors don't surface much. Sometimes they rent bunks in the lower station, but mostly they live on their rigs and guard their plots against claim-jumpers. If anyone has seen your brother, it'll be a pioneer."

She looked up with interest. "How do I know who's a pioneer?"

"Half the settlement is in the lower station right now, sweetheart." Jibby offered her his arm. "I'll take you down."

"Aren't you sailing to Paramus?" I asked.

"I'll launch later."

"But I have to go below anyway," I said. "To tell the ranger about that rig we found."

Jibby looked at me with new curiosity. "What rig?"

His ego was a flying fish cresting waves, I noted

enviously. Nothing sank him. "A prospector's by the look of it."

"It was awful inside—blood all over the walls," Gemma added with a shiver.

"Fish guts," Jibby assured her. "Happens—"

"Doubt it," I interrupted. "The Seablite Gang hauled off that rig like they had something to hide. We barely got out in time."

Jibby's gaze flew to me. "The Seablite Gang only robs government ships."

"Till now."

"Nah," he said as if convincing himself. "Prospectors got nothing worth taking."

I shrugged. "When a shark is hungry, it'll eat anything." Jibby paled, but I went on. "You know, if you're headed to the coast, you should go now. Launch later and you'll be sailing home after dark, loaded to the gills with fresh supplies. . . ."

He absorbed my words. "Nice meeting you, Gemma," he blurted, then spun on his heel and sprinted down the docking-ring. "Quit your sun soaking, boys! We gotta make wake!"

As the men on the *Seacoach* scrambled to their feet, guilt eddied through me. Hopefully I hadn't ignited mass panic just so I could be alone with a girl.

"He hardly shimmers at all," Gemma said, watching Jibby jump onto the *Seacoach*'s deck.

"He only came down two years ago."

"To stake his claim?"

I glanced at her, sure that she was teasing me for wanting to do exactly that, but she returned my look with eyes as clear as blue glass. I nodded. "In three years, Jibby will own a hundred acres."

A voice carried over the waves as the *Seacoach* pulled out of its slip. *"My Gemma lies over the ocean. My Gemma's a gem o' the sea . . ."* Jibby sang as he worked the ship's wing-sails. *"My Gemma lies over the ocean. She's such a rarity!"*

Scowling, Gemma tucked her brother's photo back into the pouch on her belt.

"Off-key?" I asked, pleased that she wasn't charmed.

"A hundred acres doesn't give him the right to be mean." She turned her frown on me as if I were in on the joke. "The world is crammed with girls like me. I get it."

I choked back a laugh. "See any other girls around here?"

She regarded me suspiciously but glanced around. "There." She nodded at the docked boats behind me. "What's your point?"

No doubt she'd spotted a floater who didn't count. A girl off a houseboat never stuck around longer than it took her parents to post mail. But when I turned, I was surprised to see a flashy yacht bobbing in the next slip. On deck, two women lounged under bright parasols.

Going by their goggles and fluttering dresses, they were from the mainland. That meant well over three hours in a boat, or more depending on the wind, just to be tourists. Normally, we were used to being alone out here, safe that what was left of "civilization" was sixty nautical miles away. But every now and then, "civilization" dropped by to take pictures.

Alarm straightened my spine. That instant, the woman in yellow spotted me and gasped, followed by the one in green, as if jaw dropping were contagious. Of course, I was facing the sun full-on, which meant my skin was catching every glint. Turning to Gemma, I whispered, "Let's tack out of here."

She pointed to a nearby hitching post. "I left our helmets in the rental sub."

"Jet-fin," I corrected automatically and thrust my mantaboard into her arms. "I'll get them and meet you on the promenade." I waved her toward the ladder, silently willing her to hurry.

But it was already too late.

CHAPTER

FOUR

It took the two women no time to clatter down the docking plank, hurrying as if I were a breaching humpback about to sink beneath the waves. With our helmets in hand, I reluctantly climbed out of the cockpit and onto the jet-fin's nose. "Excuse me." I pointed at the section of the docking-ring where they stood. "That's about as far as I can jump."

"Oh." They scuttled back to give me room, though not much.

When I landed a few feet away, their hands flew to their sun-goggles and I heard the familiar *click-click-click* of tiny levers being depressed as the women lightened their lenses. And my parents wondered why I hated visiting the stack-cities.

"You have beautiful skin," said the one in green. She sounded adult, which meant she should have known better than to gawk at a person.

"Thanks." I tried to scoot past, but the one in yellow blocked my path.

"It's real?" She slipped back her head scarf to reveal elaborately braided blond hair. "Not painted on?"

"It's real enough."

At least there were only two of them and they were women. That, I could handle. Men really triggered my adrenaline. No matter how polite or friendly, if a man stared at me too intensely or studied me like I was a curious specimen under a microscope, I'd start to choke as if my lungs had collapsed.

"I don't believe it." The woman in yellow strolled closer. "I'll bet that glimmer rubs right off."

She was teasing—I got that—but goggle-eyed and smeared in white zinc, she came off creepier than any critter out of the abyss.

"Can I try?" she asked with a smirk.

"Try?"

She peeled off one of her long gloves. "To rub it off." Her anemic hand reminded me of a sea spider as she reached for my cheek.

I forced a smile. "So long as you don't mind the fish oil."

Her fingers snapped back. "Fish oil?"

"All the pioneers bathe in it," I said, straight-faced. "So we don't dry out from living in salt water."

She gave me an appraising look. "You're making that up."

"Oh, stop being coy," the other woman snapped, thrusting several bills at me. "Now stand still and let her touch you."

"Ty!" a voice shouted. Above us on the promenade, Gemma leaned over the guardrail. "Stop showing off your skin!" she scolded loudly. To my horror, every man and woman within a hundred yards swiveled to look at us. "And don't you dare take that old bag's money!"

Muttering their indignation, the two women hurried back to their yacht.

I scrambled up the ladder to the promenade, where I found Gemma grinning widely. "That was fun!" she said.

The people lined along the guardrail were now out-and-out staring. I could live with it, but it didn't mean I liked it. Ducking my face, I headed for the tower at the center of the Surface Deck.

"What?" Gemma called after me. "No 'thank you'?"

I wasn't quite ready to maneuver through the sweaty throng of people in the market, so I waited for Gemma to catch up and then skirted the edge. But even that wasn't getting us anywhere because Gemma kept pausing to marvel over the mountains of fish piled onto tables and kneel by troughs overflowing with hairy lobsters and periwinkles. After her fifth stop, I realized it wasn't the food she was eyeing, but the crowd. She was looking for her brother.

"You're wasting your time," I told her. "Prospectors don't shop here. It's the priciest fish market in the world."

"Really?" She looked about curiously. "Why?"

"These fish were caught in the open ocean, which means they weren't swimming through what's left of the cities destroyed by the Rising." Out of the corner of my eye, I saw a cluster of shoppers pointing at me. "Can we go below now?"

I thought I'd asked it calmly, but Gemma's gaze snapped to me as if I'd collapsed in a heap. Then she noticed the gawkers circling us. "Does this happen to you all the time?" she asked.

"Only when I'm Topside."

"How do we get below?"

I pointed to the tower that was really just an elevator shaft. The only way to get there was through all of the milling people, and I couldn't spot a break in the throng. The heat, glare, and dead fish stench were getting to me. Then cool fingers entwined with mine as Gemma took the lead and plunged into the crowd, dragging me along. She barreled through the closely packed bodies, shouting "excuse me" now and then, but mostly she elbowed people aside. I held on to her hand like it was a lifeline, only to plow into her when she stopped at a hanging foot-bridge—one of many that crossed over the enormous hole in the middle of the Surface Deck. Like the spokes of a wheel, the slender bridges all led to the tower platform, suspended in the center.

"It's safe," I told her, stepping onto the titanium mesh footbridge. One story down, submarines lined the inner docking-ring. Gemma followed me while keeping a tight grip on the railing. I pointed out the white glass observatory above us, which creaked as it pivoted in the wind. "That's the ranger's station."

Inching along, she frowned at the churning water in the launch-well.

"You don't like heights?" I asked, walking backward to face her.

"I don't like falling," she said tightly, then scampered past me onto the tower platform.

When she pressed the elevator button, the doors opened into a transparent compartment with a metal column running through its center. Gemma read off the call buttons: "*Observatory, Surface, Quarters, Service, Recreation, Access*. Well," she scoffed, "those are as clear as smog."

"Observatory and Surface are the only two levels of the upper station." I pushed the SERVICE button.

As the elevator dropped out of the tower and descended through the launch-well, Gemma leaned against the flexiglass to look up at the people on the suspended footbridges. Gaining speed, the elevator zipped past the inner docking-ring and plunged beneath the waves. Gemma jumped back with a gasp, but I relaxed. Surrounded by ocean, I felt like myself again.

In silence, we plummeted through the sun-streaked water. Then she noticed the slot next to the RECREATION call button. "What's this for?"

"You have to insert an adult ID card or the elevator won't move."

"So 'recreation' is a euphemism," she guessed.

"*'Saloon and Gambling Hall'* didn't fit on the panel."

The elevator slid down the cable into the darkening blue. A swordfish glided past, attracted by the lights. "That is one huge fish," Gemma said in awe.

"And he's a baby," I replied, eyeing the six-footer. "Swordfish usually come twice as long."

With a flash of silver scales, the swordfish darted off. Gemma circled the elevator to watch it go. "I've seen more wildlife today than . . . ever." She turned her attention to a golden cloud of amberjacks. "Unless you count rats and wild dogs."

"Tell me again why people live Topside?" I teased.

Smiling ruefully, she kept her eyes on the fish. One hundred feet down, the lower station swelled beneath us, as big as a transatlantic zeppelin. The elevator slipped into the opening on top.

Two levels down, the doors opened. "Welcome to Main Street," I said as we stepped onto the Service

Deck. There wasn't a person in sight, only darkened storefronts.

She peered in window after window of the empty stores. "Why is everything closed?"

"These were never open." I led her down a hall that fanned off the central corridor. "The government thought lots of businesses would set up shop down here, but it didn't happen."

"Why not? There were hundreds of shoppers on the Surface Deck."

"It can get rough in the lower station. Make sure you head back to the mainland before nightfall, when the miners and tide-runners ship in."

"I'm not leaving until I find my brother."

I stopped. She'd said it like she meant it. "No, seriously. Today's Friday. These men live on the seafloor all week and—"

"Please. I can take care of myself. I'm tough."

Tough? If I wasn't so astounded, I would have laughed.

"Anyway, no one is going to notice me. I look like everybody's kid sister." Flicking her braid over her shoulder, she waltzed toward the transparent wall at the end of the corridor.

"Not mine." I caught up with her and decided to drop the issue for now. I'd explain how things were later, before the lower station got truly rowdy.

We turned into the outer corridor. The exterior wall was all window—smooth on the inside yet scaled outside. The large squares distorted the view only where they overlapped. Gemma paused as if admiring the ocean but then gave me a sidelong glance. "Why didn't you want that woman to touch you? She was beautiful."

I grimaced. Topsiders sure had a warped notion of beauty—like preferring skyscrapers to coral reefs. "Who cares what she looked like?" I asked as we started down the outer corridor. "I don't want to be poked by some stranger. The staring and questions are bad enough."

"What sort of questions do people ask?"

We arrived outside the meeting room. "Personal," I replied.

"Such as?"

Angry voices boomed through the closed door, which alarmed me. Town meetings didn't usually erupt into yelling matches.

"Come on," Gemma pressed. "One example."

Exasperated, I gave her one. "'Are you shimmery *everywhere*?'"

"Oh." Her eyes sparkled with mischief. "Are you?"

Without answering, I cracked the door to the meeting room and peered inside. Chairs were set up in a semicircle but lots of people stood—most wore diveskins. There were maybe fifty people inside—roughly an eighth of the total settlement population.

Though their backs were to me, I felt the tension running through the group and recognized several of my neighbors. Benton Tupper, the settlement's Commonwealth of States representative, stood on the dais, looking like an overgrown baby with his wispy hair and plump cheeks. All of the forty-five states had two representatives in the assembly to vote on the state's behalf. As a lowly territory, we got one representative, who wasn't allowed to vote, and we didn't even choose him. The assembly assigned us Benton Tupper and there was nothing we could do about it. At least he was better than no representative at all, which was what the ocean townships had. Truth was, the states didn't have it that much better. The Commonwealth only held elections for new representatives every twenty years or so. Ever since the Rising became an official catastrophe, we've lived under Emergency Law, which means certain rights get suspended. "Can't switch horses midstream," the representatives said with every cancelled election. An appropriate metaphor, considering 20 percent of the continent was now underwater.

Tupper smoothed down the sleeve of his official blue robe as he said, "Well, what do you expect? You own great tracts of land—naturally a hefty property tax comes with it."

"Hefty ain't the word for it," someone shouted, though I couldn't see who.

With a finger to my lips, I held the door open for Gemma and we slipped into the back of the room.

"Instead of complaining," Representative Tupper suggested, "you should be grateful the Commonwealth allows you to pay your taxes in crops."

"We'd rather pay in cash."

I recognized my mother's firm voice and spotted her to the left of the dais. Pa always joked that Ma looked like an Amazon, but only because of her height. She was a scientist, not a fighter. As she rose to her feet, she seemed serious, not riled. "We'd get three times as much for our crops at market than what the government says they're worth and you know it."

Next to her, Pa straddled a chair, deep in thought—his usual reaction to any problem. He ran a hand through his hair, leaving it spiked up like the prickles on a blowfish. Doc Kunze, however, who was a dozen years younger than Pa, wore an expression that more closely matched my feelings. With his long legs stretched out before him, at first glance Doc appeared relaxed, but his frown was so fierce, the corners of his mouth disappeared into the dark stubble of his beard. Even more telling, Doc massaged one scarred palm and then the other, which he only did when he was really vexed.

"Crops or cash," barked Raj Dirani as he jabbed his seaweed cigar at Representative Tupper, "either way the 'wealth is bleeding us dry." Gemma shifted nervously beside me. I supposed Raj did look pretty savage with his diveskin split open, showing off chest hair thicker than a seal's. "And what do we get for it?" he snarled. "A few lousy supplies sold wholesale, a wet-hating ranger, and a doctor who can't even make a fist—no offense, Doc."

With a wry smile, Doc tipped his hat to Raj and the assembly. It wasn't true anyway. Doc could make a fist; he just couldn't perform surgery. And it wasn't like the station's infirmary was a hospital.

"We're not getting anything wholesale," Pa said, getting to his feet. "Not lately. The Commonwealth hasn't sent us a supply of Liquigen in months. We're down to using the Trade Station's emergency stock." He waved at the dispenser in the corner with its empty glass tank. "I surely hope the lower station doesn't sink during your visit, Representative Tupper."

"As do I," Tupper replied smoothly.

Clammy fingers touched my hand. "That's a joke, right?" Gemma whispered. "The station can't really sink." Her face was whiter than a pearl and almost as shiny.

At that moment, the room lurched, which meant that down on the Access Deck some big sub had just dinged the rim of the moon pool while surfacing. Happened all the time. Gemma, however, didn't seem to know this.

"Are you going to throw up?" I asked her.

"No," she said indignantly, then considered it. "Maybe."

With my foot, I nudged the waste can closer to her.

"So, if everyone is through voicing complaints," Tupper said, "I'll get to the point of my visit."

Gemma poked my arm. "Can this place sink?"

"Yes," I whispered, "but it's nothing to fret over."

On the dais, Tupper cleared his throat loudly. "On behalf of the Commonwealth of States, I've come to ask the settlers of Benthic Territory to help in the capture of the Seablite Gang."

Noises of disbelief erupted from the crowd and the station shifted again. I heard Gemma sputter . . . but not from surprise. I hauled open the door. "There's an air blower in the hall. Stand under it. You'll feel better." With a nod, she slipped out of the room.

Someone shouted, "That's the ranger's job."

Ranger Grimes looked sweatier than usual as he pulled a pill bottle out of his pocket.

"Clearly he needs assistance." Tupper's lips held the barest smirk.

The ranger took off his hat—probably because his auburn hair was plastered to his scalp. "You try scouring the whole ocean for one stinking sub," he growled, and then pried the cap off the bottle with such force, his pills scattered across the floor. His head must have pained him something awful because he instantly dropped to his knees to collect them.

Ignoring him, Representative Tupper spread out his hands. "You're always going on about making Benthic Territory more independent. Self-governing. View this as an opportunity. This is your chance to prove that you can maintain the peace within your own settlement."

"How do you want 'em—dead or alive?" Raj asked.

Tupper smiled. "Your choice."

He'd said it so coldly he could've raised goose bumps on a corpse. I didn't like outlaws, but to hand out a death sentence so matter-of-fact felt plain wrong. And I wasn't the only one who thought so. Pa stepped forward, finally looking angry.

"And if we refuse to form a posse?" he demanded.

"There are three incentives." Tupper held up a finger, tourniqueted with a thick, gold ring. "One: The Commonwealth is halting all shipments to the settlement until the Seablite Gang is caught."

No one said anything: The announcement was not a surprise. Everyone knew the government had lost a lot of money on stolen cargo. I cracked the door and spotted Gemma standing under the blower in the hall ceiling. She gave me a feeble wave.

"Two."

I turned as Tupper raised another stubby finger

and said, "Dr. Theo Kunze has been reassigned to the mainland."

Kicking back his chair, Doc got to his feet. "Dr. Kunze is not inclined to go."

"You're a government employee, Doc," Tupper reminded him. "And not one in good standing."

Doc bowed his head. Though his dark hair hid most of his face, I saw that he'd flushed a hot shade of red. I seethed on his behalf. Everyone assumed that he had some black mark on his record. Same with the ranger. Why else would the 'wealth have assigned them to an experimental settlement? But lots of pioneers came subsea looking for a fresh start and it was understood that if a person worked hard and contributed to the community, nobody would bring up his past. Let alone in front of a crowd. For all their overblown manners and convoluted etiquette, Topsiders could be ruder than a card shark spitting chewing weed.

"I can always quit and set up a private practice down here," Doc said quietly, though his dark eyes glinted with anger.

"Not if your medical license is revoked," Tupper replied. "You'll go where you're told, Doctor." He uncurled a third finger. "Lastly, the Commonwealth will cease subsidizing new homesteads."

"No!" I cried, not caring that I was alerting the assembly to my presence. Casual as you please, Representative

Tupper had just snatched away my future. If I couldn't stake a claim subsea, what was I supposed to do? Move into a box on the Topside? I'd fare worse than a fish on the sand. Looking none too happy, Pa headed my way.

"That start-up equipment isn't a gift," Ma said, riled at long last. "It gets repaid three times over in crops or the settler forfeits his land."

"These don't have to be permanent changes," Tupper said in a soothing tone that made me want to throw a chair at him. "Since you all know the lay of the land down here, you'll flush out the Seablite Gang in no time. And once you bring them in—dead or alive—the Commonwealth will reconsider the benefits of helping Benthic Territory to flourish."

"If the settlement survives that long," I said bitterly. Pa ushered me into the hall like I was a little kid.

Gemma stood a ways down the corridor, watching a huge leatherback turtle swim past, but Pa didn't notice her. "Ty, this is important," he whispered, shutting the door behind us.

"So I heard!" *Reconsider the benefits* . . . That wasn't even a guarantee. "The 'wealth can't just change the rules and order us to hunt down outlaws."

Pa gestured for me to keep my voice down. "That's nothing you have to worry about."

"Yeah, it is. If the territory goes under before I turn eighteen—"

"Listen, I have to get back in there." He sounded hoarse, and it looked as if new lines had been etched around his mouth. "Why are you here? Did something happen?"

I hesitated. If I reported that the outlaws had likely murdered a prospector, how much more pressure would Representative Tupper put on the settlers to catch them?

"Nothing," I said. "Forget it." I'd tell my parents and the other settlers later, after Tupper had launched for the mainland.

Hand on the doorknob, Pa frowned. "You came to the Trade Station for nothing?"

Thinking fast, I said, "Gemma wants to see our homestead."

"Gemma?" Now he noticed her and his brows rose in surprise. "Hello there."

I couldn't meet her eyes. Would she scoff at the idea of wanting to see an underwater farm?

"Hi." She joined us without hesitation. "Sorry we disrupted your meeting."

Baffled by her presence, Pa looked between the two of us. "Are your parents at the market?"

"Her brother lives down here. He's a prospector," I said, opting for the simplest explanation. "Can we take the cruiser? Just for a while. I'll come back for you and

Ma," I offered, forcing myself not to fidget as Pa eyed me thoughtfully.

"We'll catch a ride with Pete," he said finally. "You two go have fun." As an afterthought, he said, "I'm glad you came subsea, Gemma."

She beamed. "Thanks."

"Ty never gets to socialize with someone like you."

"A Topsider?"

"A teenager," Pa corrected with a smile.

CHAPTER

FIVE

"You're the only kid in the whole territory?" Gemma asked yet again.

With a spin of the cruiser's wheel, I turned the big family-sized sub more sharply than necessary. "The only *teenager.* There are other kids." She was making me feel like an oddity. "Twenty-two of us."

She snorted with laughter. "If there are twenty-two girls in the shower room with me, I consider that private—look out!"

Ahead, in the midnight blue water, a shimmering wall shot out of the seabed like a geyser. I smiled at her alarm.

"That's our fence. It's charged to keep livestock in and sharks out."

"What's it made of?" Then, as the cruiser drew closer, she answered her own question. "Bubbles!"

The sub hit the dense stream of bubbles and burst through to the other side. Gemma gasped at the light, bright as a summer day on the Topside. A flurry of fish surrounded the sub and then winnowed away to reveal acres of green fields. In the distance, larger fish moved in unison over the swaying kelp, illuminated by the huge banks of lights that encircled our property. "Hot tar," she whispered, twisting to look in every direction at once.

"It's pretty great," I admitted. I was proud of what my parents had created out of the ooze, four hundred feet below the ocean's surface. Especially since people had said it couldn't be done. An unexpected tentacle of sadness wrapped around my heart. I'd picked out the land for my own homestead, measuring out the hundred acres of unclaimed terrain more times than I'd admit. The land was perfect, too—beautiful and rich with wildlife. But I couldn't think about that now. I pointed at a shoal of pinkish red fish. "We have a side venture selling perch, but mainly we farm kelp and plankton."

"Plankton?"

"Our meadow is up on the ocean surface." Still she looked baffled, so I added, "You eat plankton every day. That green cream added to your food, what did you think it was made of?"

"Not plankton."

Just then a tiny, glowing shrimp shot out of the jet spray of bubbles and onto the sub's viewport.

"Look," Gemma exclaimed. "It's a gem o' the ocean."

"Yep," I confirmed. "It was sucked up by the air jet and got the ride of its life."

"Oh!" she cried as a cyclone of bright blue fish whirled past, and she climbed into the backseat to follow them. "You don't eat those, do you?"

"No. Ma keeps them just for pretty. 'Like flowers in a garden,' she says."

"But they're tropical fish." Gemma spilled back into her seat. "How can they live this deep?"

"Seawater is the same, deep or shallow. We just warm it up and add light and oxygen. The bubbles"—I pointed at the fence, which appeared silvery from this side—"keep in the heat." When I glanced over and found her studying me, I tensed.

Flushing, she mumbled, "Your skin is distracting." She pointed at the floating platform across the field. "What are those cages for?"

I leaned back from the control panel, knowing that its blue light made the fluorescent particles in my skin shimmer. At least she'd said *distracting* and not *creepy*. I steered the cruiser toward the platform lined with cages and basins. "Lobsters." I named the contents of each container we crossed. "Crabs. Shri—" Gemma's gasp cut me off. "What?"

Frantically, she pointed at the far end of the farm. "Look at that jellyfish!"

I couldn't help but laugh. "That's our house." It *did* look like an enormous jellyfish with its tentacles dangling into the kelp—if jellyfish grew big as blue whales.

Gemma gaped. "Your house? But it's mushy!"

"I know. Your skyscrapers have hard walls and sit in the dirt. But it's different down here. A building needs some give. The smaller ones are outerbuildings where we keep our goats and chickens."

"You raise farm animals as well as fish?"

"Not to sell. We keep them for the milk and eggs." Which reminded me I still had chores to do.

As we approached the giant undulating bell that was my home, Gemma's expression softened. "It's beautiful."

"Pa modeled all the houses down here after deep-sea invertebrates. Mostly different kinds of jellyfish. Those shapes work better in water."

"Your father designed all the buildings in Benthic Territory?"

"A lot of them." Did she think I was bragging? I felt compelled to explain. "My parents were part of the research team that built the first homestead. Ma's specialty is aquaculture, which is a fancy way to say *deep-sea farming*."

We pulled up alongside my home. Transparent plastic wrapped the floating house, while honeycombed walls, filled with foamed metal, gave the building shape. I steered the cruiser past a large window and pointed at the room inside. "See? We don't live much different from you."

Gemma shot me a look. "Yes, we all have fish swimming outside our windows."

"Besides that." I dropped the sub through a school of red snapper.

"Besides that, your house is exactly like any stack-city apartment. Except it's bigger than one room," she continued, loading on the irony. "And not crammed into a concrete tower covered with doomsday graffiti."

"They can't all be that bad."

"Some have two rooms," she quipped, then turned serious. "Most people live on the affordable floors below the moving walkways and train tubes, so everything is shadowy." She gazed at the expanse of green. "We're the ones who are the Dark Life."

Under the house, a crop reaper was moored in a hangar. I pushed an icon on the control board and the cruiser rose toward the large glowing hole in the bottom of the house. "It's a moon pool," I replied to her questioning look. "The air in the house is pressurized to keep the sea from flooding in."

We surfaced inside the large, circular room. The ocean was dimly visible through the metal foam walls, giving the wet room a watery glow.

"I still don't get it," Gemma said. "Why doesn't the pool overflow?"

"Ever turn a bucket upside down and push it underwater?" I popped the cruiser's hatch and then looked back to see her nod. "Our house is the bucket," I explained as I balanced on the sub's sloped hull. "The air trapped inside keeps the water at a certain level."

"Until the bucket tips," Gemma said nervously as she stood up in the hatch and looked around.

"Our house doesn't tip," I assured her. "The anchor chains keep it balanced and they're tethered to pylons in the seafloor." Overhead, a catwalk circled the room. Had we arrived in one of my family's two minisubs, I would have used the clamp to hoist the sub out of the water. But the cruiser was too big to store inside. "By the way," I said as I leapt to the moon pool's submerged ledge. "We don't like being called Dark Life."

"Because you don't really live in the dark?" She eyed the sliver of water between the bumper and the ledge.

"No. Because it's a science term for bacteria that can live without light. We're not bacteria." I headed across the wet room, adding, "Just jump," without looking back.

In the mechanicals room, I scanned the banks of monitors, checking the numbers—pressure, atmosphere, and temperature—getting the pulse of my home. I heard Gemma leap onto the ledge of the moon pool with a splash. Satisfied that the house was in working order, I rejoined her and showed her where to stow her helmet, gloves, and boots. Then I snapped our Liquigen packs into slots in the wall, explaining, "They'll refill automatically."

As I clicked on the viewphone to check for messages, Gemma wandered across the wet room. "Why does one family need so much space?"

I smiled at the judgment in her tone. Unlike light and air, we didn't need to import space. "Vehicles, for one thing." The equipment bay alone took up the whole right side of the wet room. "The med-shower is over there." I pointed toward a door on the left. "In the changing room. You better check your vitals."

Gemma was more interested in the enormous window on the opposite side of the moon pool. Behind the glass, a jungle bloomed. "It's a greenhouse, isn't it?" she asked. There was a splash by the cruiser. She jerked around. "What was that?"

"My sister probably. I better warn her about you." As I knelt by the moon pool, Gemma hastened to my side. I turned my attention to the shadows beneath the house, but Zoe wasn't climbing up the ladder. "What the heck?"

As Gemma bent, putting her hands on her knees, something whipped by the dangling ladder. "What was that?" she gasped.

"Darned if I know." I leaned in for a better look, only to have the moon pool erupt with spray, which sent me sprawling back with a splash. I glanced up to see a hideous snakelike creature rising out of the water. Its eyes were yellow slits and a red fin crested its head like a bloody blade. I scuttled back while Gemma grabbed me by the arm, trying to drag me away. For a split second, the creature hovered above us. Then it shot forward, jaws wide, as it lunged for me.

The sea serpent's jaws dropped toward my thigh and connected hard. I winced, expecting to feel searing pain as its teeth pierced my skin—but the pain never came. Instead of rising with its prize in its maw, the creature's head lolled in my lap. Dead.

"Come on, pull him up!" a muffled voice yelled. I looked up to see a small figure in a green diveskin scramble over the edge of the moon pool. Of course it was Zoe. "Don't be such a baby, Ty," she said, unhinging her helmet. "He can't hurt you."

I shot her a dirty look, but she just sent her helmet skittering across the floor. "For light's sake." I pushed the red-finned head out of my lap and stood. "Warn me next time you shove some dead critter up at me."

Ignoring me, Zoe shook out her messy curls and peeled off her dive gloves. Those, she threw across the room. Nowhere near her gear locker. When she unfastened the basket at her waist, I snapped, "Don't dump it out here." But it was too late: She sent dead fish sliding every which way, including one flounder, which skidded into the toe of Gemma's boot. Zoe's eyes followed the boot upward and she yelped in surprise.

"You drag home sea monsters and the sight of her"—I hooked my thumb at Gemma—"makes you jump?"

"Hi. I'm Gemma." She waved, though she continued to gaze curiously at the sea serpent lying half out of the moon pool. Zoe had given us both a fright, yet Gemma seemed to have bounced back already. I had to give it to her — she was resilient.

"That's Zoe."

Thankfully, Gemma didn't stare at her. My sister, however, blatantly gaped at Gemma with her lips forming a perfect O until I put a finger under her chin and closed her mouth. "She's nine," I said, as if that excused gawking. "So what is this thing anyway?" I asked Zoe as I nudged the silver-skinned snake thing with my foot. "And where'd you find it?" I was curious, but I also knew that when my sister started talking about some creature, everything else slipped from her mind.

Sure enough, she looked adoringly at the limp sea serpent. "He's an oarfish, Ty. Really rare. Help me get the rest of him inside."

It wasn't exactly what I was itching to do — but I grasped the oarfish by the head and dragged it out of the moon pool. Its snakelike body coiled once around the wet room, yet it kept coming. I pulled out nearly fifty feet of it before reaching its tail. The entire time, Zoe danced around the oarfish, bending now and then to pet it.

"Your sister is so beautiful," Gemma whispered to me. "She looks like an —"

"Angel?" I asked, tossing the oarfish's tail aside.

She flushed. "You've heard it before."

"Once or twice," I admitted. Though I didn't get why she was embarrassed. Even other settlers, who were used to kids with shimmering skin, got tricked into thinking that Zoe was angelic because of her wide eyes and blond curls. Then they got to know her.

"Hey, shrimp," I called, "where're you going to put this hunk of meat?"

"He's not for eating," she snapped. "I'm going to keep him."

I groaned. "Zoe, it's dead. Probably rotten. It'll stink up the place."

Gemma dropped to her knees and gave the oarfish a sniff. "It's not rotten," she called.

Across the room, something twitched. The flounder, which had been lying still, was now flopping around. "And that isn't dead," I said.

One by one, other fish quivered and then, like mouse-traps set off in unison, they all thrashed to life. My eyes met Gemma's. The alarming thought that dropped into my mind had obviously dropped into hers: Maybe the oarfish wasn't dead, either.

Gemma scrambled to her feet just as the creature awoke, flailing and snapping its jaws.

CHAPTER

SIX

Gemma danced back from the thrashing oarfish while I bounded over its coils, running for the weapons rack. Harpooning the wriggling thing would be next to impossible, so I grabbed the shockprod. Whirling, I unsnapped the prod's safety lock. But before I could touch the electrified tip to the oarfish, Zoe slammed into me. "Don't you hurt him!"

I tried to dodge to the left, so she dodged left. When she threw herself between me and the oarfish a third time, nearly brushing the tip of the shockprod, I lost all patience. "Zoe, get out of the way." I shoved her aside but instead of stumbling back, she dropped to the floor and wrapped herself around my leg.

Try as I might, I couldn't shake her off. Like a dead weight, she anchored me to the spot, while hollering, "I caught him. He's mine."

Across the room, Gemma leapt from bench to bench, trying to stay ahead of the flailing oarfish and its snapping mouth.

"Gemma!" I threw her the prod, hoping she knew enough not to touch the electrified tip.

She caught it with both hands. "Which end?" Without waiting for the answer, she jabbed the prod at the oarfish as if trying to stab it to death, only she kept missing because the creature never stopped writhing. At least she'd chosen the correct end to point down.

Zoe scrambled to her feet. "Stop it!" As she started across the room, I caught her around the middle and hoisted her off the floor. She thrashed even harder than the oarfish, which had finally found its way to the moon pool.

"No!" Zoe cried as the creature slid into the water, uncoiling as it went. With a solid kick to my shin, she wiggled out of my hold and slid after the oarfish, but before she could close her fingers around its tail, the oarfish vanished, leaving only a ripple on the moon pool's surface. With a wail of frustration, Zoe ran to the window to watch it snake over the kelp. Then she turned on me. "I'm going to tell Pa you pushed and grabbed me."

"Go ahead," I said as the tension drained out of me. "Just make sure you tell him why."

I crossed to Gemma, who was now doubly armed as she brandished her green knife, along with the shockprod.

"Do you have moments like this every day?" She handed over the prod.

"Often enough," I admitted, studying her knife.

She held it up. "My brother sent it to me."

"He found it on the seafloor?"

"Yes," she said excitedly, offering it to me. "It's ancient. It's Mayan."

I nodded, not surprised. "The subsea landslides that dumped the old East Coast into the deep also uncovered a lot." I handed the knife back to her. "It's a keeper."

"Richard wrote that it was carved from a single piece of jade and used for—"

"He knows," Zoe interrupted.

Surprised, Gemma looked from her back to me.

"Human sacrifices," I finished, then frowned at Zoe. "It's rude to interrupt someone."

As usual, she ignored me. "Wait till you see Ty's room."

"She doesn't want to see—"

"Yes, I do!" Gemma cut in. "I know. It's rude to interrupt someone. But I want to see everything!"

Zoe's smile was triumphant. "Follow me."

"Not till you pick up the fish," I said, but she bounded up the stairs that curved along the outer wall. "You know I'm in charge when Ma and Pa aren't here," I shouted as she disappeared. Grinding my teeth, I grabbed a bucket. "Go ahead," I told Gemma. "I'll be up in a minute."

She hesitated, staring at the fish flopping across the floor.

Maybe she thought that leaving them out of the water was cruel. "They're going to die anyway." I tossed a mackerel into the bucket. "Zoe feeds them to her pets."

When Gemma lifted her gaze, her expression wasn't disgusted but puzzled. "There's not a mark on them. How did Zoe catch them? She didn't have a net."

I knelt to scoop up more fish, avoiding her eyes. "She sets traps."

"She caught the oarfish in a trap?" Gemma looked skeptical. "Why was it stunned?"

I didn't have a ready answer for that. Luckily, Zoe appeared on the stairs. "Gemma, don't you want to see Ty's room? He's got three jade knives just like yours."

I frowned. Zoe could only know that if she'd invaded my room on some other occasion.

Gemma cast me a curious look, then followed Zoe upstairs.

It took me a while to pick up the fish, but when I finally got to the second floor, I saw that the girls had yet to make it into my room. Gemma must have asked about everything along the way. Now she was examining the kitchen sink, which had three spigots. "Hot, cold, and salt," Zoe explained with impatience. "Come on."

"But why do you need salt water inside?" Gemma asked.

"It keeps the food fresh," I answered, coming up behind them. I pointed to the tanks of live fish and squid shelved along the wall.

Gemma nodded but didn't say anything. However, when Zoe opened the door to my room (something I wouldn't have allowed any other day), she responded with pure awe. "Hot tar," she whispered. "Is it all yours?"

Now that she was in my room, I wished I could hustle her out of it. My walls were lined with shelves, crammed with treasure I'd dug out of the seafloor. There were daggers and rings, axes and chalices, nautical tools and even a polished brass dive helmet. Necklaces and amulets hung from the posts of my bed, while primitive stone deities flanked the large window. Suddenly my hobby seemed greedy and obsessive.

"Ty collected all of it himself." Zoe twirled with her arms outstretched.

"It's not mine," I said in answer to Gemma's question. "No one can own this stuff. I just restore it and then ship it to museums."

"I wish the girls at the boarding home could see this." Gemma stopped by the shelf that held a dozen crowns and looked back at me. "Can I touch one?"

"Take your pick," I said. She selected a gold crown studded with rubies. *Spanish, 1400s*, my brain ticked off automatically.

Zoe stopped twirling. "What's a boarding home?"

"It's where parents send their kids once they turn six. That is, if the family can afford it. The 'wealth pays my board."

"People send their kids away?" Zoe asked. It was one of the few times I'd ever seen my sister look horrified.

"Parents come visit on weekends and holidays." Glancing up from the crown, Gemma caught Zoe's pitying expression. "Everyone does it." She placed the crown on her head. "Really, boarding homes aren't bad. The one I'm in now has a gymnasium and a library." She turned to me. "Do you have a mirror?"

I touched the dimmer switch by my door and nodded toward the window. The glass darkened until it reflected the room.

"Glacial." Her smile widened. "Amazing how that works."

"The house computer controls it."

"Not the window. The crown." She beamed at her reflection. "It makes you look special."

My stomach turned over. Why would anyone want to look special? It was just a polite way of saying different, which was only slightly better than being called a freak outright.

"Don't you want to live with your family?" Zoe asked.

I shot her a silencing look.

"My brother is the only family I have," Gemma replied. "And I do want to live with him." She pulled a folded paper out of the pouch on her belt. "See this? It's an emancipation form. Once Richard signs it, I'm in charge of my own life. No one can tell me what to do or where to go."

"I need one of those," I joked.

She ran her finger over the signature line. "That's why I have to find him."

"Just write in his name," Zoe suggested. "No one would know."

"Ms. Spinner would." Gemma tucked the emancipation form back into her pouch. "She has his signature on file."

"Was he a ward of the 'wealth, too?" I asked.

"Until he was eighteen." She took off the crown. "You can make it a window again."

I reversed the dimmer switch. When the mirror brightened, Gemma gasped. Something large and dark hurtled toward us. It smashed into the flexiglass, jarring the house, and sent us tumbling to the floor.

As soon as I got to my feet, I pressed against the window and tried to see where the thing had gone. Zoe nudged me aside to look out, too. "What was that?"

"Hewitt." I spun and offered Gemma a hand up.

She got up without my help. "What's a Hewitt?"

"Our neighbor."

"Why'd he hit the house?" Zoe yelled after me as I tore out of the bedroom. "That was dumb."

Whatever his reason, I knew it wouldn't be good.

CHAPTER SEVEN

A dive helmet broke the surface of the moon pool as I slid across the wet room floor. "What's up?" I asked as Hewitt Peavey crawled out of the water. Flopping onto the floor, he tried to talk before he'd cleared his lungs of Liquigen — not a good idea. "Breathe," I advised, unsnapping his helmet.

Hewitt was twelve, but his panic made him look younger. His hazel eyes were wide with fear and his shine, which usually made his brown skin gleam like polished copper, was now ashen. "Outlaws," he choked out.

Fear hit me like a one-two punch. "At your homestead?"

"They knocked out Pops." Tears filled Hewitt's eyes.

"The outlaws only attack supply ships," Zoe argued as she crowded in beside me.

I knew better, but rather than admit it, I shoved the helmet at her, saying, "Stow it," and helped Hewitt to his feet. "Go on."

"Pops was in an outerbuilding, talking to me on-screen, when this white thing just appeared out of nowhere. A man."

"Shade," I whispered.

"I didn't have time to warn Pops. He got hit so fast. Then the whole farm went black." Hewitt sounded as if he still couldn't believe it.

"But just for a second, right?" I said. "Then the backup generator kicked on."

"No. It's still dark. Ma sent me here to fetch your pa. She's tending to Pops. She thinks he's only unconscious, not . . ." He didn't finish the sentence.

The whole farm was still dark? I couldn't fathom it. Everything on the homesteads—from the air jets that created the wall of bubbles to the water heaters and blowers—ran off generators powered by scalding water from rock chimneys on the seafloor miles away. The black smokers didn't just stop spouting hot water. But what were the chances of both of a homestead's generators breaking down at the same time? It had to have been sabotage. Without power, the Peaveys' livestock would escape. Worse, their house would collapse.

"Who's Shade?" Gemma asked from behind me.

"The leader of the Seablite Gang," I said. And the only gang member who didn't darken the glass of his dive helmet during robberies. He would just appear out of nowhere, according to his victims.

"He's albino," Zoe added, clearly eager to share the frightful details. "An albino with a shine. Anyone who's seen him says his skin is so bright your eyeballs get burnt just looking— "

"Zoe, call Pa and tell him to get over to the Peaveys'." I dug into my locker for my helmet. Luckily, I hadn't changed out of my diveskin. "Pa is coming from the Trade Station," I told Hewitt. "It'll take him over half an hour."

"But we have only sixteen minutes and thirty-six seconds left!" His corkscrew hair stuck up every which way. "Mixed with frigid water, the water around the homestead, heated to seventy-one degrees, will chill down in thirty-two minutes. . . ."

I didn't know how fast a hundred acres would chill, but I wasn't going to argue about math right now. I pried a fresh Liquigen pack from a slot in the wall.

"You're going over there?" Zoe asked.

"Shurl will need help." I snapped the pack into my diveskin, just over my heart, and inserted the tube that attached to the mouthpiece in my helmet.

"There's nothing you can do," she argued. "You're not Pa."

"Just call him."

"He'll tell you not to go."

She was right. "Call Doc first," I amended. "Tell him Lars is hurt and that he should come here. We're closer than the infirmary. And toss me a prod."

Hewitt cast a longing look at Gemma. "You smell like the Topside."

Flustered, she turned to me. "Calling someone a Topsider is an insult, isn't it?"

"Not to Hewitt," I replied, pushing the seams of my diveskin together. Instantly the material melded into an invisible closure.

Sinking to the floor, he rested his chin on his fists. "Buildings don't deflate up there."

"I'll go with you." Gemma scooped up her gloves and helmet.

"You can't," I said as Zoe threw me a shockprod. If it weren't so cumbersome, I'd have taken our biggest harpoon gun. "The outlaws might be there."

"They *are* there," Hewitt said.

Ripping open her diveskin, Gemma snapped in a Liquigen pack. "I'm not scared of outlaws."

"You should be," Zoe said as she pressed the graphics on the viewphone. "They'll skin you alive, pop out your eyeballs, and make you dance."

"Where did you hear that?" I demanded.

"Nowhere. I made it up," she admitted. "But it could be true."

"Ty, maybe she's got the bends," Hewitt said, tipping his head at Gemma.

"I'm a Topsider. That doesn't mean I'm totally useless." She stepped into my path. "You'll need help."

Yeah. Lots of it, I thought. I glanced at Hewitt huddled on the floor and dread winnowed through me. I had no idea what I was headed into. Maybe I *could* use her help.

"Okay, come," I relented, stepping onto the lip of the moon pool. "We'll take the reaper."

"Doc says don't go," Zoe yelled from across the room.

On-screen, Doc shouted, "Ty, wait for your pa."

I sealed my helmet to muffle his words.

"You only have fifteen minutes," Hewitt warned.

Gemma joined me on the edge of the moon pool. "What happens after fifteen minutes?"

"Everything dies." With that, I sucked in a cold blast of Liquigen and dropped into the water.

CHAPTER

EIGHT

"Look out!" Gemma yelled when a school of tuna enveloped the reaper.

Frenzied, the fish blocked my view out the window as they tried to stay in the light. I snapped off the reaper's high beams and as fast as the fish had appeared, they darted off. I should have cut the lights sooner. Who knew if the Seablite Gang was still around? A pair of dolphins swam by, clicking warning. I checked the control panel. The seawater was warm—too warm for the ocean floor. We must have crossed over the Peaveys' property line.

In the distance, pinpricks of red beckoned—the battery-powered emergency lights had kicked on. I sped toward the Peaveys' house, which looked like a giant octopus tethered to the seafloor by its tentacles. Its sagging sides told me that the internal supply of pressurized air had dropped. If I didn't get the power on soon, their house would deflate and then flood. The plummeting water temperature would kill their schools of warm-water fish, the mahimahi and snapper. The rest would escape without the bubble fence to keep them in. Hewitt's family could lose everything.

With a nod toward the viewport, I said, "Keep an eye out for the *Specter.* The outlaws' submarine. You saw it from below. Straight on, it looks like an oversized great white shark."

"With its mouth open?" she asked.

"Yeah," I said, surprised.

"And a big black bubble caught in its throat?" She pointed at a looming gray shape to our left.

The *Specter*! I reversed the throttle and shot the reaper backward, like a retreating squid. Hopefully, by cutting the lights, I'd kept the outlaws from noticing the tubby block of a sub. Shoving the throttle down, I put the reaper into a nosedive, burying her in the thirty-foot-tall kelp.

An instant later, the *Specter* glided over us as supple as a real shark and ten times as big. The bridge was set in the sub's craw—a black bubble of flexiglass. And somewhere inside was Shade, an outlaw more ghost than man.

Gemma clasped a hand to her mouth. I followed her horrified gaze to the *Specter*'s caudal fin, where a rotting corpse was chained. "They say he was a member of the gang who betrayed Shade."

"Why doesn't someone arrest them?"

"The Commonwealth gave *us* that job." I couldn't keep the bitterness out of my voice. As if settlers—people like my parents—could round up the Seablite Gang.

Representative Tupper was out of his mind. "The ranger has never found the gang's hideout, which makes it kinda hard to arrest them. Some people think they live on the *Specter* all the time."

"I'd go dinghy if I never got off it."

"Her. A sub's a ship and ships are always female. Anyway, cutting up a prospector isn't dinghy?" I watched the *Specter* disappear into the blue.

"Let's follow them!"

"I've got to help Shurl and Lars." I maneuvered the reaper out of the kelp. "Now."

"I can do that. You should tail the outlaws and find out where their hideout is."

"I'm not tailing them." I sped the reaper toward the sinking house.

"Why? Are you scared?"

"Yeah," I replied, without a twinge of shame.

"I'm not."

"That's because you haven't heard the stories." I pointed at the house in front of us. "Besides, see how the top floor is slumping? Hewitt's home is losing air by the second. Now look around, see all the drifting fish? They're dying because the water is getting too cold for them. I don't know how to turn the power back on, but there might be something else we can do."

"You're right," she admitted, giving me a sidelong look.

"I don't want to be right," I muttered as I aimed the reaper toward the large hole on the underbelly of the house. "I want this not to be happening." The moon pool itself was dark, but the red emergency lights outlined it. I cut the reaper's motor just as we broke the water's surface next to the Peaveys' sub.

When I cracked the hatch, a fierce voice greeted me. "Don't move. I've got a harpistol aimed right at you." I peered through the shadows to see the handgun inches from my forehead, with its barrel of mini harpoons fully loaded. Round-faced and angry, Shurl looked like a ferocious version of the one doll Zoe owned but never played with.

"It's me, Shurl." I put my hands up so she wouldn't shoot me.

"Ty!" She holstered the harpistol, much to my relief. "Did you see them?" she asked as I climbed out of the reaper. "The Seablite Gang?"

"They were leaving." Balanced on the ledge of the moon pool, I looked uneasily at the buckling walls.

"Is your pa on his way?"

"He won't get here in time."

"You shouldn't have come, Ty," Shurl scolded. "It's too—"

"We want to help," Gemma said, popping up in the open hatch so suddenly that Shurl stumbled back.

"That's Gemma," I explained, while above me the ceiling puckered like a deflated balloon.

"I have to get the animals!" Shurl spun on her heel and ran off.

"Shurl, the house is coming down!"

She headed for the enormous window on the opposite end of the wet room. "I can't leave them."

I raced after her, wondering why she didn't keep her goats and chickens in an outerbuilding like all the other settlers. When I stepped into the greenhouse, a chicken flew against my legs.

Distressed goats crowded around Shurl, bleating loudly. "It's okay. Mama's here." Clucking, she scooped up a chicken. "We can't afford to replace them."

As if she'd leave them behind if she were loaded with money? Not a chance. "We can take some in the reaper." I hefted a goat into my arms and backed out of the greenhouse. "Where's Lars?"

With a hen under each arm, Shurl followed me. "I got him from the outerbuilding." She scurried to the sub floating next to the reaper. "I had a heck of a time lifting him into the sub. Good thing he's so skinny." There was a catch in her voice.

Only Shurl would describe Lars as skinny. Through the sub's viewport, I saw him slumped across the pilot bench. Hewitt's parents were a study in opposites: Shurl tiny and dark-skinned, Lars plump and pale. Now blood matted Lars's thinning blond hair. He was a proud man. It made me sick to see him brought so low by some chum-sucking outlaw.

"Is he unconscious?" I asked.

Shurl nodded. "He's stopped bleeding but—" She was drowned out by squawking chickens, which flapped madly as she dropped them down the sub's hatch. Through the viewport, I saw the birds land on Lars, who didn't move.

"Ty," Gemma called, "give me the"—squinting, she studied the goat in my arms—"whatever it is."

She'd never seen a goat before? I jogged to the reaper, only to stumble and skid as the house dipped, sloshing water over the rim of the moon pool. Gemma lost her perch on the edge of the hatch but appeared again instantly. The girl did have guts. I leapt onto the bumper, swung the kicking, bleating goat into her arms, and then followed Shurl back into the greenhouse. We loaded most of the animals into the reaper within minutes. Not that we had any minutes left if Hewitt's calculations were right. Too bad we couldn't save the Peaveys' fish by piling them into the reaper as well.

As I handed over the last of the chickens to Gemma, Shurl gazed around the wet room. "Up until the deflating, it was a good home."

The far wall crumpled like a wad of aluminum foil in a giant fist. "Get Lars out of here," I urged Shurl. "Take him to my homestead. Doc will meet you there."

"There's one more goat. . . ."

"I'll get the goat. You go."

With a grateful nod, she dropped into the pilot seat beside Lars. I waited for her sub to disappear beneath the roiling water before running back into the greenhouse for the last goat. As I grabbed it by a horn, a loud ripping noise stopped me cold. Something on the second floor was tearing. With my heart drumming in my ears, I dragged the goat across the wet room.

The reaper rocked as I clambered onto it, goat in arms. "Do you think you can drive this thing?" I asked Gemma as we forced the goat down the hatch.

"Sure," she replied with what sounded like false confidence.

"The navigation system will take you back to my homestead. Just hit *home* once you get clear of the house. I'm going to see what the outlaws did to the generator." I slammed the hatch shut. "Take her down."

Across the room, the ceiling collapsed onto the floor. I leapt off the reaper and ran to snatch a mantaboard from the wall. The room tipped, sending dive equipment and scooters sliding across the wet room. Cabinets burst open, their contents flying out. Something sharp nicked my ear as I hopped and dodged the loose gear. Through the viewport I saw Gemma scanning the control panel while shooing chickens out of her lap. Colored lights played over her face as she studied the holographic controls floating in front of her.

Yelling wouldn't help, but I wished she'd hurry. I flipped my helmet closed and sucked in Liquigen. Behind me, the acrylic glass wall of the greenhouse tore free of the ceiling, teetered, and crashed to the wet room floor. Finally, the reaper sank out of view. With the mantaboard over my shoulder, I jumped into the moon pool and dropped through the churning water.

Around me, tether chains plummeted in slack loops as the house came down. I saw Gemma piloting the reaper feverishly among the falling coils. She banked and twisted. A length of chain slammed onto the back of the reaper, but she managed to speed clear of the house.

I followed, fighting my way through the reaper's wake of bubbles until I was out from under the house. Behind me, it collapsed like a dying beast, creating a swirl of water that dragged me to the seafloor.

When the silt finally settled, I turned on my helmet's crown lights and faced the wreckage that had been the Peaveys' home. Streams of escaping bubbles marked its descent into the ooze.

I hugged Hewitt's mantaboard. Maybe the outlaws

weren't behind the bloodbath in the derelict sub, but they sure as heck did this. My temper boiled. As if the settlers weren't already breaking their backs to keep their homesteads running, raising fish and shellfish for Topsider dinner plates and creating crops out of mud—a gang of lazy, no-good outlaws had to turn all this hard work into a dead harvest?

Confused fish knocked into me on all sides. Dolphins, which had stopped by for an easy meal, were now calling out to one another to get moving. Soon the big predators would arrive, attracted by the tremors of the dying fish. If I didn't zip out of here pronto, I'd end up on the chewing end of a feeding frenzy. Still, I couldn't leave without at least trying to get the power back on. Maybe the problem could be easily fixed. Or maybe a mermaid would swim by and offer me her assistance. . . . The odds were as good.

Using my crown lights, I found the power cable that led from the buckled house into the kelp field. The screen on my wrist displayed the outside water temperature, which had dropped lower than the tropical fish could tolerate. If they weren't dead yet, they would be soon. I hopped aboard the manta and followed the cable into the field, heading for the main generator.

Ahead of me, the kelp shook. Something large was moving through the stalks, crossing the field. I cut the manta's motor and slipped to the seafloor. Clipping the tether to my belt, I let the board hover and drew out my shockprod. I couldn't see past all the kelp, but I could tell that whatever was plowing through it had picked up speed. In a panic, I kicked backward only to realize I'd gone beyond the edge of the field and was now out in the open. Exposed.

The kelp in front of me thrashed with life. But as the last green stalks were thrust aside, a shoal of dead fish swirled between me and the field, blocking my view. I swept at them, knowing that their scattered bodies weren't dense enough to hide me. The lifeless fish bounced away and I glimpsed something large hovering before me. Before I could grasp what it was, the farm exploded with light.

The power was back on.

I shielded my eyes and blinked, trying to adjust to the sunlamps as fast as I could. I parted the fingers I held over my helmet, only to recoil in horror. A corpse towered over me, still in its diveskin. Blanched and bloated.

Revolted, I kicked back a few feet, then paused to look again. The swollen arms and oversized chest meant it had been dead for a while. Not *it*, I told myself. But thinking of it as human grew harder as the body floated closer to me. Inside the helmet, the dead man's pallid, hairless head gleamed as if lamprey eels had sucked out every drop of his blood. His skin was whiter than white. Except for his eyes, which were entirely black. The pupils, irises, whites—all black. Like gaping holes in his skull.

Suddenly, an icy wave of understanding broke over me. That wasn't bloat but muscle. And I wasn't face-to-face with a corpse. I should be so lucky. No, the horrifying visage in front of me belonged to Shade, the leader of the Seablite Gang. And he was very much alive.

CHAPTER

NINE

I jerked backward, kicking fast. The outlaw didn't follow. Head cocked, he seemed to be assessing whether I was worth troubling himself over. More dead fish swirled between us, blocking Shade from view. I yanked down the mantaboard and heaved myself onto it, driven by the image of his sightless eyes.

No, not sightless. Shade wasn't blind. Those must've been dark lenses.

The current sent the drifting fish upward. I twisted to look back but saw only the kelp field. Gunning the manta, I headed for home. The power was back on; there was no reason to stay. Hopefully the crops would survive the drop in temperature. The lights illuminated a few half-eaten fish, swirling in the currents—all that remained of the Peaveys' livestock. All gone, through escape or death.

Slowly, fear drained out of me and my rage returned. The Seablite Gang could have just taken the supplies they wanted. They didn't have to destroy the Peaveys' house and farm—everything Shurl and Lars had created out of nothing. I slowed the manta. Gemma was right. If I followed Shade and learned the location of the gang's hideout, Ranger Grimes could arrest the whole lot of them. Then Representative Tupper would "reconsider the benefits of helping Benthic Territory to flourish." It was us against them, simple as that. Settlers against outlaws. I looped back to the field.

The swaying stalks were easy enough to spot. I stayed low over the kelp and followed the movement. Shade plowed toward the edge of the field. The bubble fence, marking the end of the Peaveys' property, lay beyond. The end of the continental shelf was another mile east and it was a heck of a drop off from there. In most places, the shelf sloped gently down to the abyssal plain. But not behind the Peavey property. Hewitt and I had cruised along the edge many times. It was a rocky sea cliff that plummeted into the darkness of the abyssal plain, which was nearly two miles below the ocean's surface. Plenty of sea caves pockmarked the face of that cliff. Maybe one of them was where the outlaws moored the *Specter.*

Still hovering, I propped myself on my elbows to watch the outlaw exit the field. Inside the dome of flexiglass that was his helmet, the back of Shade's bald head glowed an unearthly white. Then he stepped through the bubble fence, and I noticed the harpoon gun strapped to his back. Exactly the size I'd found too cumbersome to bring along. How I wished I had it now.

Ma and Pa would hate this plan, but they weren't here. With the bitter taste of adrenaline rising in my throat, I revved the manta and shot through the wall of bubbles. On the other side, the sea was cobalt blue and featureless. In the distance, I made out a faint glow. Not the greenish bioluminescent light of a sea creature, but the warm glow from the crown lights of a helmet.

I tailed Shade until, without warning, the glow vanished like a snuffed matchstick. I veered to the right. Had he guessed that I was trailing in his wake? Slowing the manta, I circled around, but before I could even begin my search for him, light blasted me. There stood Shade, boots planted wide on the seafloor, crown lights on bright, hefting the jumbo-sized harpoon launcher. Spotting me, he lifted his gun and took aim.

I reared the manta, but not high enough. A harpoon smashed into the bottom of the board, nearly jarring my teeth from my jaws with its impact. Wheeling about, I revved the manta to make my escape, but instead of leaping in response, the board sputtered. I jammed the handgrips to the highest speed, yet I jerked to a full stop. Cutting the motor, I tried restarting it, which seemed to work. The manta shimmied to life under my body, but then it plowed backward through the water.

As hard as I twisted the grips, I couldn't get the board to respond, let alone stop. Wiggling forward, I tipped my head over the edge. A harpoon jutted from the manta's underside, wobbling in the water's drag—no surprise there. But I hadn't realized the spear was attached to a chain. Flipping onto my back, I sat up and saw Shade putting one hand over the other, drawing in his catch like a reanimated corpse, bloodless and black-eyed.

I kicked myself free of the manta and swam upward, pausing only to flick the button that released my fins from my boots. Unless Shade dropped his harpoon launcher, he'd never catch up to me. His size worked against him, even without the weight of his gun pulling him down. Still, I leveled out and kept swimming. Now horizontal.

Eventually, my muscles ached from exertion. I slowed and dropped to the seafloor, checking around me as I went. There was no telltale glow of a helmet light anywhere—only endless midnight blue water.

CHAPTER TEN

"Of all the reckless, dangerous things I've ever heard!" Ma cried, running across the wet room. "You should have waited for us!"

I rolled off the rim of the moon pool and onto the floor, exhausted from my long slog home. Hauling me to my feet, she went on, "The outlaws might have seen you!" She unfastened my helmet, nearly taking off my head along with it. "Shurl said the *Specter* was still on the property when you got there. What in the great ocean possessed you to go over there without me or Pa?"

"Let him catch his breath, Carolyn," Doc Kunze said, coming up behind her.

I sucked in air. If Ma was this upset about me simply going to the Peaveys', no way was I going to mention meeting up with Shade. "Pa wouldn't have made it in time," I told her. "Is Gemma here?"

"She sure is." Doc didn't smile, but his dark eyes glinted like he was on the verge of it. "Shurl said she couldn't have saved the animals without you two, so she's cooking you up a feast."

Taking a seat on the bench, I tugged off my dive boots. I couldn't think about food. Since coming face-to-face with Shade, my stomach had stayed coiled tight. "I'm getting dressed," I announced.

Of course, Ma didn't take the hint. Arms crossed, she said, "Pa is still off tinkering with the Peaveys' generators, trying to figure out what went wrong, so exactly how did you get home?"

I hesitated. If I admitted that I swam the whole way, I'd hear about it for the next fifty years. "A mantaboard." When she frowned, I added, "I had a prod and my dive knife."

"When you're gripping a board, you can't fend off a great white."

"Come on, Carolyn," Doc said. "No shark's gonna get a bite off him. Your boy is faster than a torpedo. Besides"—he clapped me on the shoulder—"you're forgetting Ty can practically see in the dark. He just maneuvers around the sharks. Don't you?"

I didn't dare reply, so I got busy toweling off my diveskin.

"Dinner's almost ready," Ma said quietly. "Come up when you're dressed." She headed upstairs and I nearly fell off the bench from surprise. Yeah, I'd hoped to avoid a lecture or worse, but now that I had, I was spooked. At least she should have thrown out a we'll-discuss-this-later.

Doc's medical case thumped onto the bench next to me, sweeping Ma from my mind. Just the sight of that metal briefcase made me choke. I sprang to my feet, ready to outrun any rising memories. "I appreciate you coming to my defense, Doc," I said in as normal a voice as I could muster. "But I'm fine."

"Settle down. I'm just checking your vitals."

I dug my nails into my palms to give myself something to concentrate on. "Doesn't Lars need you?"

"I stitched him up and gave him something to help him sleep. His pride is wounded, but he'll live."

When Doc cracked open his medical case, the stench of antiseptic filled my head. The gauze and steel instruments gave off a scent as well—probably too faint for most people but it sickened me.

"You haven't had an exam since I came to the territory four years ago," Doc said. "Your parents ought to get you checked out every year, especially since you're living subsea." He scooped up a health scanner. "Relax. You won't feel a thing."

"No!" The word lashed out, more aggressive than I'd intended. I wasn't about to let any doctor examine me. Not even one that was a family friend.

He studied me, dark brows lifted with surprise, then tossed the scanner back into the case. "Okay . . ."

I snatched clothes from my locker, letting the silence between us stretch. If Doc thought he was going to get an explanation, he was sorely mistaken.

"You know you can trust me, Ty."

His cautious tone turned up the flame under my already simmering mood. I wasn't some skittish kid who'd just spit out my medicine.

"If there's anything you want to tell me," he went on, "you know I can't repeat it to anyone without your permission."

"Yeah, you can." I split open my diveskin. "I'm not eighteen."

"But I wouldn't."

I peeled down my diveskin as far as my hips, then paused and shot him a pointed look.

A wry smile curled over his mouth. "Yeah, I got the hint." He snapped the medical case closed. "See you upstairs."

I focused on taking in air, listening as he crossed the wet room. When his boots started up the stairs, I unclenched my fists, only to hear Doc stop short.

"Ty, if you're going to tell your ma that you came home on a mantaboard," he advised, "make sure you've got one with you. Next time, she might notice that you don't."

Only after his footsteps faded upstairs did I sink to the bench, panic still lodged in my chest.

I found the other nonadults in Zoe's room. Their backs were to me, but I could see that all three were dripping with artifacts from my collection. Hewitt, armed with a sword and ebony crossbow, had also strapped on a golden chest plate. Gemma, who was peering into one of Zoe's aquariums, sported armbands and the Spanish crown that she'd admired earlier. Of course Zoe was the worst. She'd taken full advantage of my absence and had swathed herself in every piece of jewelry she could find—a tiara, necklaces, and a jeweled girdle. Under the weight of all the precious metal and gemstones, it was a wonder she could stay upright. Before I could complain, Gemma turned to Zoe and said, "Your room is amazing."

At least hers looked obsessive, too. Tanks of sea life sat on every surface and were built into the walls. Her bed had a shark's jaw for a headrail and pieces of fifty varieties of coral hung from the ceiling. Even her window was an aquarium. She'd set up a feeding station outside of it so that fish hovered there all the time.

"How come this tank is all black?" Gemma asked.

"Those guys like living in the dark." A mischievous gleam came into Zoe's eyes. "Want to see them?"

In the doorway, I smiled when Gemma nodded, knowing where this was headed.

Zoe strolled over to the wall switch next to the tank. "I'll turn on a blue light so you can see them. But you have to lean in real close."

When Gemma bent forward, hands on her knees, Zoe flipped the switch. As the tank lit up, a ghoulish fish face popped into view. Its teeth looked like jagged shards of glass and its eyes bulged red. Only a pane of glass separated the viperfish's gaping jaws from Gemma's nose. Yelping, she scrambled back, making Zoe grin. In the eerie blue light, a dozen fearsome fish hovered: vampire squid, gulper eels, snaggletooths, and loosejaws.

"I caught them down on the abyssal plain." Zoe traced a finger lovingly across the glass. "They look mean but they're real delicate."

A smidge of pride welled in me. My sister had amassed an incredible collection of rare specimens. Even Ma, who had a knack with living things, didn't know how she managed to keep them all alive. "Love" was Ma's best guess.

Zoe plucked a mackerel out of a bucket. "Want to see the viperfish eat?"

"No!"

Despite Gemma's answer, Zoe opened a slot above the tank. She threw in the wiggling mackerel and set off a feeding frenzy. Gemma and Hewitt howled with revulsion, which made me laugh. Zoe was too busy gazing at her precious monsters to notice the rest of us. As

Gemma spun away from the tank, she caught sight of me, flashing me a smile that was so bright, heat seared through me.

"Your sister doesn't look so much like an angel anymore," Gemma said, coming over to me.

"And you haven't even seen her out in the shark cage, chumming up the water."

"I hope you don't mind." She touched the crown on her head self-consciously. "We were trying to make Hewitt feel better."

I glanced at Hewitt, who did look happy, encased in gold. "It was a good idea," I said.

"You should have seen Ma when she heard you went to the Peaveys' knowing the outlaws were there," Zoe chortled.

"She turned into a real black smoker," Hewitt said sympathetically.

"If Gemma and I hadn't gone, your family would have lost a lot of your animals."

"That's what Ma said." Hewitt took off the crossbow. "But your ma thinks you're worth more than a goat. Don't know why."

"You'll be skimming algae for a month," Zoe predicted gleefully.

"Skimming algae?" Gemma asked.

I shrugged. "Stuff grows on the house, so we have to scrape it off by hand."

"It's slimy," Zoe said, clearly enjoying herself. "And takes forever. Your fingers cramp up."

"That's another thing better on the Topside." Hewitt flopped onto Zoe's bed. "You never have to scrape scum off your house."

"We don't have houses," Gemma corrected.

"Right!" Hewitt sat up. "You all get to live together. Can you imagine it? Everywhere you look there are other people. You plunge outside—"

"Plunge?" Gemma asked.

"Dive, whatever. There's always someone to talk to. It would be great to have that many neighbors."

Zoe stopped feeding her pets to listen.

"My boarding home takes up two floors in a seventy-five-story building with over a thousand apartments in it," Gemma said. "All those people aren't exactly neighbors."

"Of course," Hewitt agreed. "It's more like one big family all living together. No one ever gets lonely up there," he said, turning to Zoe. "They don't even know what the word means because they never need to use it."

Gemma leaned into me. "Is he for real?"

"'Fraid so."

Oblivious, Hewitt went on. "You never have to do anything alone. There's always someone to help catch dinner. Or harvest the kelp."

Gemma looked like she'd just been poked with a shockprod.

"Hewitt doesn't get Topside very often," I explained in a low voice.

Hewitt heard me. "Never!" He pounded a fist on the mattress. "I *never* get to go Topside!"

"Because you run away the second your foot touches land," I replied. "Last time, you busted into a stranger's apartment and scared the air out of some woman."

"I called out hello," Hewitt said defensively. "I don't know why she started hollering."

"Maybe because she was in her underwear." I had gotten all the details from an account a humiliated Shurl gave my mother.

Hewitt crossed his arms, disgruntled. "I just wanted to see the inside of a Topside apartment."

In the distance, a sub powered over the kelp field, shooting out a trail of bubbles as it neared the house.

"Pa's home," Zoe squealed.

"The power is up and running steady," Pa said, ripping open his diveskin as if he couldn't wait to shed it. I stowed his helmet for him. "How is Lars?"

"He'll be fine," Shurl called on her way down the stairs. "When we got here, Doc was waiting for us, thanks to Ty's quick thinking." She squared her shoulders. "Give me the bad news, John."

"They didn't take much as far as I can tell. Just food and Liquigen. Your crops should recover."

"What about the livestock?"

Pa shook his head. "Gone. But we've got plenty to spare. If all the families give you thirty fish, you'll get your schools up to a good size by next year."

"The house?"

"We only need four people to get it reinflated. We can do it tonight," Pa assured her. "That'll give the inside a chance to dry out. Then tomorrow, we'll give it a thorough cleaning and it'll be good as new, you'll see."

She nodded, fighting back tears. "Come on, then. Dinner's on."

As we headed for the stairs, I felt Pa's hand, warm and heavy, on my shoulder. "You did a man's job today, Ty. I'm real proud of you."

If you knew I followed a dangerous outlaw into the open ocean alone, I thought, *you might not be so proud.*

Dinner felt like a holiday between the company and everyone being all decked out. As soon as Shurl had seen Hewitt and the girls in their finery, she'd insisted that everyone put on an artifact from my collection. "We're all alive and we're together. We even have a special guest," she said, smiling at Gemma. "Tonight is a celebration."

All the adults obliged. Ma selected a rope of pearls she'd "always had her eye on"; Doc chose a scabbard and sword; and Pa put on a medallion. Poor Lars slept through the whole thing. "I'll help you clean and retag everything," Ma whispered to me as we returned to the dining room and took our seats.

"It's okay," I said, though I hadn't chosen a piece for myself. Until the Seablite Gang was caught, I didn't feel like celebrating anything.

Outside, the giant lamps that surrounded the property were beginning to dim, simulating nightfall. Doc pulled out Gemma's chair for her. "Are you heading back to the mainland tonight, young lady?"

"No. I'm going to stay in Benthic Territory for a while."

"Who are you staying with?" Ma asked, setting a platter heaped with steaming lobsters onto the table.

"No one," Gemma said cheerfully. "I'm going to rent a berth at the Trade Station."

Everyone froze. If only I had known that was her plan, I would have nixed it right off.

"In the Hive?" Doc asked, dropping into his chair.

Pa frowned. "I thought your brother lived in Benthic Territory."

Gemma nodded, answering both questions at once. "But I haven't found him yet." I was glad she didn't try and tell Pa how tough she was.

"What about your parents?" Shurl asked.

"I don't have any."

Ma and Shurl exchanged a pained look.

"Is there someone else responsible for you?" Ma asked gently.

"Ms. Spinner, the boarding home director. But when Richard sent me money to come live with him, she signed my emancipation form." Gemma pointed at the serving bowl in front of her. "Is that the fish that makes your skin shimmery?"

"No," I said. "Monkfish isn't bioluminescent."

Gemma's shoulders slumped.

"You want a shine?" Hewitt asked with disbelief.

"Who wouldn't?"

"The Hive doesn't rent berths to anyone under eighteen. Do they, Theo?" Ma asked Doc while passing him a bowl of crispy calamari.

"Nope," he agreed, heaping food onto his plate. "It's against Trade Station rules. Only prospectors and miners bunk there."

"That's where the prospectors hang out?" Gemma asked excitedly.

"When they're pearl rich," Shurl said, cracking Hewitt's lobster for him. "They trade manganese nodules for cash. Then they spend it all on cards and booze."

Ma put her hand over Gemma's. "You're welcome to stay with us until you find your brother."

"I'd like that. Thank you." She glanced at me, which made me feel hot and restless, so I concentrated on spooning jellied crab onto my seaweed salad.

"You can sleep in my room," Zoe offered. Gemma seemed less thrilled by that prospect.

"Great," Hewitt muttered. "I get to sleep in Ty's museum."

"I left my duffel bag with all my stuff at the Trade Station," Gemma said. "In a rented locker."

"Ty will take you to get it in the morning," Ma assured her.

"How did the outlaws do it, John?" Doc asked, pouring himself a goblet of sea grape wine. "Turn off the Peaveys' power. I thought that couldn't happen."

"So did I," Pa said ruefully. "Near as I can tell, an electromagnetic pulse shut it all down. But I don't know how they generated it."

"If Ranger Grimes puts together a posse," I said, "I want to be part of it."

"Not even if he pins a gold star to your chest," Ma said firmly.

"That wet-hating ranger isn't going to take a posse into the deep," Doc scoffed, with a wave of his knife. "The man can't even swim. He's the one who should be reassigned to the mainland, not me."

A lobster claw clattered onto Shurl's plate. "You're leaving?"

"At the end of the week," Doc said resentfully. "I don't have a choice."

"If the settlers . . . I mean *when* the settlers arrest the Seablite Gang, you can come back, right?" I asked.

"Arrest the . . . What?" Shurl looked from one person to the next.

"We've been assigned an impossible job." Pa set down his goblet. "It makes no sense. The government has been pressuring us for years to expand our farms, grow more crops, breed more fish. And now the 'wealth is pulling its support over a gang of outlaws? There are plenty of desperados sailing the ocean. What's so special about the Seablite Gang?"

Doc shrugged. "How long can the settlement last without imported supplies?"

"A week, maybe two," Pa said grimly.

"No," Shurl gasped. "We have plenty of food and—"

"After today's meeting, every last drop of Liquigen was siphoned out of the Trade Station," Pa explained. "The settlers panicked because without it, we can't stay outside long enough to get any real work done."

"We can buy Liquigen on the mainland," I said.

"And pay full price?" Shurl asked forlornly. "Every dime we make goes toward taxes. If we can't buy wholesale, we can't buy."

"Then there's equipment," Pa went on. "If a diveskin

or air purifier fails, we can't even afford to repair it, forget replacing it."

"Supplies and equipment are the least of it." Ma tossed her napkin onto the table. "Once word gets out that the Seablite Gang sank a homestead today, a lot of settlers will think long and hard about moving back to the Topside." Picking up her plate, she left the dining room.

Not us. She couldn't possibly mean our family. I looked to Pa, but when he offered no reassurance, I felt my future sink into the abyss, where it was bleak and unfathomable.

CHAPTER

ELEVEN

Holding tight to an anchor chain, I struggled to attach it to a spike embedded deep in the seafloor. The Peaveys' house had inflated quickly once Pa turned on the pressurized air pumps. Nearby, Gemma gamely held on to her chain even though she was floating on her tiptoes. I hid my smile as I watched her collapse into the muck to keep from getting pulled off her feet. I touched her arm to show her that I'd secured the end of her chain. Releasing it, she cheered silently as her section of the house rose into place. Good as new.

The dark interior of the Peaveys' home was another story. In the few hours that the house had lain on the seafloor, small creatures had found their way inside. Now crabs scuttled underfoot, illuminated by the strips of emergency lights embedded in the floor. Small fish darted in the boot-deep water while Zoe splashed around, trying to catch a blue stingray.

"Why didn't everything get crushed when the house came down?" Gemma asked me. "Like the lockers."

"When a house deflates, it sinks. But it never collapses all the way," I explained, hanging a battery-operated lantern on a wall hook. "There's a skeleton of support girders to keep that from happening. And on the inside, everything—the walls, those lockers, the cabinets upstairs—they're all made from flexible materials. So even if something gets squashed, it bounces back into shape."

"Your father must be very smart."

"He didn't work alone. When they built the first homestead, he and my ma lived on a big research sub for over two years with lots of other engineers and scientists. That's how my parents met."

"Can't we turn on the lights?" Hewitt asked loudly.

"No, let all the water drain out," Doc advised, hooking a lantern on the dangling vehicle clamp. "I know the lights are sealed, but why take a chance on someone getting a nasty shock?"

I was glad that Doc had volunteered to come and that Ma had stayed home with Lars. Despite his scarred hands, Doc proved helpful in getting the house reinflated. But more important, Ma wouldn't have reacted well to the dripping ceilings and general wreckage. Equipment jutted out of the shallow water like the toppled buildings at the seashore that hadn't gotten swept into Coldsleep Canyon.

"Let's get the fans going," Pa said, hooking up another lantern. "We'll do the real cleanup tomorrow, when things are dry. Tonight, just take care of whatever can't wait."

As I led the other kids upstairs and into the kitchen, a chill settled into my bones. Hot water from a seafloor geyser was flowing through the pipes in the floor again; I could hear the faint gurgle. But the pumped-in water had yet to warm up the air inside the house. The walls of the usually cheery kitchen were dark and moist and water dripped from the ceiling. In grim silence, Gemma and Hewitt wiped down the counters and floor, which were slimed with algae and dying sea creatures from the cracked aquariums. Zoe frantically filled bowls and buckets with seawater. "Hold this," she said, thrusting a pot into Gemma's hands. When Zoe scooped a red speckled octopus off the floor and dumped it into the pot, Gemma made a face.

"He won't hurt you," Zoe scolded.

Gemma looked around for a place to put the pot, but the kitchen counter was lined with other makeshift aquariums. Just as I was about to offer to take it, the octopus poked a tentacle out of the water and coiled it around Gemma's wrist. With a shriek, she sent the pot flying but the octopus didn't go along for the ride. It clung to her wrist, despite her frantic efforts to shake it off.

"Hold still." I scrambled to help her. "I'll get it."

Panicking, Gemma whipped her arm back and forth until the octopus sailed across the room and splatted against the wall. With a cry, Zoe ran to it. Tenderly she gathered up the mollusk and then scowled at Gemma. "You could have hurt him."

"Hurt him?" Gemma sputtered. "That snot-rag with eyeballs grabbed me!"

In unison, Hewitt and I sucked in air. Slowly, furiously, Zoe got to her feet, still cradling the octopus.

"No!" I yelled, stowing Gemma behind me.

Hewitt scrambled on top of the kitchen table. "Get out of the water!"

"Zoe, calm down," I said, trying to sound reasonable in the face of my sister's rage. "Gemma can't help it. She's a *Topsider.*"

Gemma poked me in the back.

"She doesn't know how cool sea creatures are," I went on. "It's not her fault."

Zoe considered my words and then, after shooting Gemma a withering look, she stalked out of the kitchen with the octopus clinging to her like a baby. I relaxed a fraction.

Still standing on the table, Hewitt glared at Gemma. "Are you crazy? Never make Zoe mad. Ever."

"What is with you two?" Gemma asked.

"Zoe doesn't fight fair," I muttered.

"Please," she said with a snort. "Last year, I lived in a dorm with over a hundred teenage girls. The tears alone rivaled the Rising. Never mind the fights. I think I can handle one nine-year-old."

"You're tough. I know." I exchanged a look with Hewitt, who clearly had the same thought in his mind:

In a tangle with Zoe, tough didn't matter.

We retreated to the damp living room, where we pulled chairs around a portable heater, trying to stay warm while ignoring the constant dripping. "I don't know why she's bothering to save the plants in the greenhouse," Hewitt muttered. "We should just move Topside."

Zoe joined us, still holding the octopus, though she'd transferred it to a water-filled vase. She scowled at Gemma, who was rubbing her hands together over the squat heater. Hewitt cast another disgruntled look at the stairs that Shurl had just descended, carrying rods for propping up plants in the greenhouse.

"Your parents aren't going to move over a little house sinking," I said, dropping into the chair next to Gemma.

"The Seablite Gang attacked us!"

"Are they called the Seablite Gang because they're a blight on the sea?" Gemma asked.

"Yes," Hewitt said vehemently and then paused. "What's a blight?"

"Actually"—Doc set down a bucket of rags as he entered the living room—"they escaped from a prison named Seablite."

I looked up with surprise. "Where'd you hear that?"

"I was working for the Department of New Solutions at the time. We were trying to solve the housing problem. This was before my professional reputation got put through a meat grinder." He'd said it lightly, but his smile was strained. "My job was to monitor the health of anyone living in experimental housing. This happened in Seablite." He held up his palms, each marred with a slash of a scar. "By way of an inmate's knife."

Zoe hopped up for a closer look. I stayed put. Years ago, Doc had told me how he'd gotten his scars and that he couldn't perform surgery anymore because all the tendons had been severed—but he'd never mentioned the prison's name.

"Representative Tupper is pressuring us to catch escaped *convicts*?" I asked. Disbelief and disgust churned in my stomach.

"And not just any convicts." Doc pulled up a chair. "These men are so dangerous and damaged, they were locked up in an experimental prison."

"Experimental?" Gemma asked.

"Seablite was the first and only subsea prison ever built," Doc said, then turned to me. "You've probably piloted over it a thousand times."

"What?" I asked, incredulous. "Where is it?"

"Between here and the Trade Station. It's the building that used to house a science lab. At least, that's what the public was told."

"The one marked 'structurally unsound'?" I asked. The squat two-story building was so nondescript, I'd never paid it much attention.

"That's the one," Doc confirmed.

My indignation flared. "Why'd the 'wealth call it a science lab?"

Doc raised an eyebrow. "What do you think the settlers would've done if they'd known the government had built a maximum-security prison within territory boundaries?"

His question was ironic but I answered anyway. "They would have protested." Why did government deception still surprise me?

"Time to go," Pa called from the doorway.

"Wait," Zoe cried. "I want to hear about the breakout."

"What breakout?" Shurl asked, coming up beside Pa, carrying a potted tomato plant.

"The Seablite Gang isn't just a bunch of outlaws," Hewitt told her. "Doc says they're escaped psychos and that we're not safe down—"

"How'd they do it, Doc?" I asked, interrupting Hewitt. "Escape?"

Pa and Shurl joined our circle—clearly curious as well.

"Well, that's the eerie part." Doc leaned back in his chair, with his eyes on the flickering light inside the heater. "No one knows. The power in the whole prison just shut down one night—like what happened here. But also, the guards fell into a deep sleep. They weren't drugged; I checked them later."

"I bet the outlaws bashed them all over the head," Zoe said.

"I don't think so," Doc said, remaining serious. "The guards didn't have a mark on them. Not a bump, not a bruise. And every one said he felt fine when he woke—exactly twenty minutes later. Their eyes opened in unison. They didn't even realize the prisoners were gone at first. The door to the main holding cell was still sealed. And there were two more locked doors after that. Not scuffed in any way."

Everyone leaned forward, listening intently, our faces glowing with the orange light.

"And the surveillance cameras . . . that was strange," Doc said softly. "The cameras recorded static for exactly twenty minutes, then resumed filming again as if nothing had happened."

Shurl looked shaken. "This is just a spooky story, right, Doc? To scare the kids."

"It's all true." He held up a scarred palm as if taking an oath. "Five years ago, the Seablite Gang vanished from behind bars and no one has ever figured out how they did it."

Gemma's eyes lit up. "Maybe one of them has a Dark Gift. Or they all do. They were living underwater, right?"

"I've considered it," Doc told Gemma. "Maybe during their time subsea they developed unknown abilities."

Pa stood, annoyed. "Stories like that start rumors."

"If they were in prison, they were adults," I said. "That stupid theory only applies to kids."

"What if it isn't just a theory?" Doc asked. "No one has ever come up with a better explanation for how the outlaws escaped." He focused on Zoe. "How about you, angel? Got a special trick to show us?"

To my horror, Zoe slid her gaze to me as if asking for my permission. Of course, everyone followed her look.

"Forget what I've been saying, shrimp." I kept my tone light, though I wanted to strangle her. "You have a real special gift. No reason to keep it a secret."

Hewitt's mouth fell open.

"Really?" Zoe asked.

"Sure," I said. "Why not? Show them what you can do. But don't blame me when everyone starts screaming."

For once in her life, Zoe squirmed as all the attention was directed at her.

"What can she do?" Doc sat forward.

I shrugged. "Not many people know that she can . . . pick her nose with her tongue."

Hewitt and Gemma yowled while Pa laughed outright.

"See? I told you no one wanted to know about it." I pinned my sister with a hard look. "Some abilities you keep to yourself."

Doc was the only one who hadn't recoiled. He was studying Zoe thoughtfully. Too thoughtfully. I caught her attention and tipped my head fractionally toward Doc. She pasted on a smile, oozing innocence as she stuck out her unusually long tongue and touched it to the tip of her nose. A chorus of "Don't," "Stop," and "No" rang out from around the circle. Doc settled back with a forced smile.

Twenty minutes later, suited in my diveskin and helmet, I swam to a feeding station under one of the Peaveys' outer-buildings. Everyone else sat in the cruiser, which hovered over the kelp. I dumped the bag of unusable food we'd pulled from the kitchen into the mesh-topped bin. Sadly, the Peaveys had no fish left to feed, but the crabs would eat it. They'd eat anything.

As I stroked back toward the cruiser, I saw Gemma peering out the rear viewport. Spotting me, she started to wave but then paused. Her lips parted with surprise as she pointed at something beyond me. When she shouted over her shoulder to the others in the cruiser, I whirled to see what had alarmed her.

By the boundary lamps at the far end of the Peaveys' homestead, a bulky dark shape floated over the kelp. A chill skipped down my spine. Were the outlaws back?

The mysterious shape drifted closer. It was a sub all right, but not nearly big enough to be the *Specter.* Like a shadow, the sub slipped sideways over the field. Caught in a current. Gliding haphazardly . . . derelict.

If I'd wondered where the outlaws had hauled the abandoned, bloody sub . . . I now had my answer.

CHAPTER

TWELVE

"I was going to tell you about the rig this afternoon," I explained to Pa over the sound of the shower, "but you'd just gotten bad news from Representative Tupper. . . ." My words rolled away.

It wasn't an accident that Pa decided to have our "talk" now. The med-shower, with its health sensors built into the interior walls, was like a walk-in lie detector. No doubt Pa had stationed himself right by the computer screen outside of the stall to check how fast my heart was beating with each answer I gave.

"That doesn't matter," Pa said through the frosted glass door. "You still should have told us. That sub needs to be towed to the Trade Station. And Doc has to run tests to find out if all that blood came from a human."

Ignoring the tiny dancing red lights of the sensors, I turned off the water, took my towel from a hook inside the stall, and wrapped it around my waist. When I stepped out, Pa was right where I'd figured—next to the computer screen—watching my blood pressure rise.

"I don't want you keeping things from us. Not for any reason. Now, do you have anything else to tell me?"

"The sub wasn't by the Peaveys' this morning," I admitted, knowing that sooner or later he'd think to ask where we'd found the rig originally. "It was down by Coldsleep Canyon."

The muscle in Pa's jaw ticked. "You went off the shelf alone?"

"Yeah, but that's not the point, Pa." Seeing that my father was about to argue that indeed that was the point, I said hurriedly, "A derelict sub wouldn't drift up the continental slope. It couldn't. The outlaws must have towed it up the slope to the Peaveys'."

"And why would they do that?"

"They wanted us to find it." Conviction had me feeling bold. "If they didn't, why not leave the rig by the canyon? No one goes down there."

"Except you, clearly."

"I can take care of myself. Better than you give me credit for." I strode across the changing room and grabbed another towel to dry my hair. I braced myself for the chewing out that was sure to come.

"If you're right," Pa said softly, "and the *Specter* brought this rig up to the continental shelf—well, there had to have been a reason. We just don't know what it is. Some say the outlaws are crazy. But I don't think so. Something's going on, and it can't be good."

"Maybe it'll come clear when Doc figures out whose blood it is."

Pa gave me a hard look. "There's nothing else I should know, is there?"

There was, of course. But I shook my head. I'd dropped enough bombs for one night.

Having changed into drawstring pants and a T-shirt, I opened the door to my bedroom and was surprised to find the lights on and Hewitt sitting up in his sleeping bag even though he'd gone to bed over an hour ago. The reason became clear when I noticed Gemma on my bed, swinging her feet.

"Zoe snores," she explained.

She was wearing one of Zoe's nightgowns, which was too short on her. I averted my gaze, only to notice that Hewitt had strapped the golden chest plate over his pajamas. "You can't sleep in that," I said.

Reluctantly, he handed it over. As I reshelved it, I stole another glance at Gemma. Did girls really walk around with their legs showing long ago? I'd seen pictures taken before the Rising, but I still found it hard to believe. Forget what the New Puritans said about the morality of it; any girl living Topside now would land herself in the hospital with third-degree burns if she exposed that much skin to the sun.

"So, have you heard of him?" she asked Hewitt, continuing a conversation that my arrival had interrupted.

"That's the kid the Topsiders wrote about, right?" Hewitt asked, plucking at his pillow. No doubt to avoid meeting my eyes. "The one with biosonar?"

"I thought you were tired," I said to him.

"What's biosonar?" Gemma asked.

"Same thing as sonar"—Hewitt shimmied into his sleeping bag—"only it's an animal sending out the signal, not a machine."

She frowned. "What signal?"

I dimmed the room light. "It's getting late."

After a loud yawn, Hewitt mumbled his reply. "The clicking noise dolphins and whales make."

"Yes, that's what Akai does. Then he listens for the echoes and his brain somehow turns them into pictures." She slid off the bed. "So, do you know him?"

"No." He lay back in his sleeping bag.

"You know," I said gruffly, "the doctor who wrote that article admitted that he never actually examined or even met a kid named Akai. He based his whole Dark Gift theory on old case notes."

"He studied other kids," she countered.

"An outright lie. He said he did research on teenage boys down here. But four years ago, when that stupid article came out, there weren't any teenagers in Benthic Territory."

"Can we talk somewhere else?" Gemma strolled over to me. "Alone," she added softly.

Uncomfortable, I ran a hand over the back of my neck the way Pa did when he wanted to think about his answer. How many more questions could she have about Akai and Dark Gifts? "Sure," I said finally.

Her expression turned indignant, though I couldn't begin to guess what I'd done wrong this time.

"It sure took you long enough to decide," Hewitt piped in.

Was that it? "Not because of you," I told Gemma. "I don't mind being alone with you."

"Never mind. Forget I asked." She turned to leave.

I caught up and barred the doorway with my arm. "I had to think of somewhere we can go."

Quietly, I led Gemma past the kitchen. I heard my parents talking softly in the living room. All that separated us from them was the opaque wall of the stairwell. Before I could even make out Ma's words, her tone told me she was riled up.

I waved Gemma down the stairs ahead of me.

"The outlaws nearly killed Lars today." Ma kept her voice low, but it crackled with anger. I didn't have to peer around the corner to know that her hands were on her hips and her eyes were shooting sparks.

"Who knows what happened inside that derelict sub. The territory isn't safe anymore and you know it, John."

Gemma descended halfway down the stairs, then noticed I hadn't followed. I needed to hear Pa's reply.

"It was never safe, Carolyn," he said, sounding weary. "But what's worse? Living with the threat of danger or living safe and secure with no land to call our own? Is that what you want for our kids? To be hemmed in by millions of other people, without room to explore or dream?"

"Our dream is failing," Ma said sharply. "Instead of settlers, we get drunks and gamblers passing through. And outlaws who steal from hardworking folk." She grew angrier with each word. "What if Ty had gotten trapped inside the house when it collapsed today?"

I gritted my teeth. When was she going to realize I wasn't a little kid anymore? I could swim better than both of them and sense danger faster. And I sure as heck could judge when a house was about to cave in.

"Subsea houses don't come down that fast," Pa replied. "There's always time to get out."

Ma made an exasperated noise while Gemma's beckoning grew more insistent. I considered bursting into the living room and offering to scrape scum off the house for the next decade if my parents would just get off this topic.

"I don't want to raise my children in a place where there's no doctor," Ma whispered fiercely. "Not when Ty ignores our rules and takes more risks every day—like exploring derelict subs."

I winced. I should have known she wasn't going to let that misdeed slide by. Oblivious to the hushed argument in the next room, Gemma headed back up the steps. As she passed me, I caught her hand and pressed a finger to my lips.

"So that's it?" Pa snapped. "You want to abandon everything we've worked for? Give up?"

I waited for Ma's reply, but when her footsteps clipped halfway across the living room, I realized she wasn't going to answer him. She was walking away from the argument—heading directly for us. Dragging Gemma halfway down the stairs, I pressed us both to the wall. Ma stormed by the stairwell without looking down. I relaxed, only to realize I'd flattened Gemma against the wall with an arm across her chest. "Sorry!" I whispered, releasing her.

She hurried down the stairs. This time I followed her, Ma's comment about ignoring rules ringing in my ears.

As soon as I closed the greenhouse door behind us, Gemma asked, "Will you help me sneak into the Saloon? I want to see if my brother is there."

"What? No!" I sputtered. "Did you hear anything my mother just said? If I break another rule, she's hauling our whole family Topside."

"At least you'd be together."

"Yeah, all crammed into one room. Sounds like heaven."

Gemma's brows drew together. "I can't even remember my parents. And I haven't seen my brother in three years. If we could all be together, I wouldn't care if we lived in a closet." She marched past me and disappeared into the foliage.

Okay, now I felt like total chum. "You'll get kicked out of the Saloon faster than a card shark can shuffle." I pushed through the stalks of corn to find her. "No one will let you step off the elevator unless you're eighteen."

She stopped shoving through the plants. "Not twenty-one?"

"Like I said, you can start a homestead at eighteen. They consider you an adult then."

"I look eighteen."

"Yeah, and I don't know how to swim."

"I bet you could get me in."

"No," I said firmly. She didn't know what she was asking. She hadn't seen the knife fights I'd witnessed on the Service Deck alone.

Gemma sat on a tank of filtered water by a large window. Apple trees, ripe with fruit, swayed overhead. "I didn't have permission to come to Benthic Territory," she said.

I wasn't surprised to hear it. Already I knew that Gemma wasn't the kind of girl who asked permission.

"You ran away?" I said.

She nodded as she traced a starfish that was climbing the window. "The director, Ms. Spinner, is probably bursting an artery right now." Gemma's smile was grim. "She wants a bigger apartment. But every time a kid goes missing from her boarding home, she gets dropped down the housing waiting list, which is really demeaning to an adult. Space being the ultimate status symbol. Anyway, I go missing a lot, so Ms. Spinner's chances of moving get worse and worse. Most of the time, I just sneak up to the tower roof. It's broiling hot and smells like tar, but it's the only place where I don't feel trapped."

I understood what it meant to feel trapped, only the whole Topside made me feel that way. A sun-baked roof would be just another cranny in hell.

Gemma met my eyes. "Ms. Spinner said if I disappeared again, she'd send me to a reformatory for juvenile delinquents."

"Just for looking for your brother?" I asked skeptically.

"She sent Richard away for less. All he did was sneak into a quality-time room after hours."

"A what?"

"You sure don't know much about life *Above*." She gave the ceiling a disparaging wave. "When parents come to see their kids, they rent a quality-time room with couches and games and a kitchen. When I was younger, I'd spend every Saturday walking up and down the visitors' hall, peeking in the windows. I'd pretend I was shopping for a family."

My throat constricted at the image of her alone in a corridor that rang with other people's talk and laughter.

"Anyway," she went on, "sometimes late at night, Richard would pick the lock on one of the rooms and I'd meet him there. I was really little, but I always managed to sneak out of whatever dorm I was in. We'd eat together and he'd read to me—like other families. Then we'd clean up so no one would know we'd been there. Richard made that part fun, too."

"Why couldn't you meet in one of those rooms during the day?"

"We didn't have money. That's why, when we got caught, Ms. Spinner called Richard a thief. He stole space—a serious offense. So she shipped him off to a reformatory and wouldn't tell me which one." Gemma's voice cracked but her eyes remained dry.

Did Gemma blame herself? "I'll bet he never regretted spending the time with you," I said.

She shrugged like she wasn't so sure. "I didn't hear from him for four years. Finally, when he was eighteen, they let him out."

"Was he different?"

"He used to laugh a lot, but he hardly smiled at all when he came back. After six months, he took off. Said he couldn't stand the crowds. I think that's why he ended up down here." She touched my arm. "Ty, please. Help me find him."

How was I supposed to say no to that?

CHAPTER

THIRTEEN

"When I said I'd help you, I didn't mean this," I whispered angrily. We were on the Service Deck, standing in front of the elevator shaft that ran down the center of the Trade Station. I wanted to help her find her brother but had a sneaking suspicion I might ruin my own life in the process.

"You promised," she reminded me. "Anyway, it's day. The Saloon is going to be empty. We should have snuck out last night."

"Day. Night. Doesn't matter. The Rec Deck will be packed. The miners and tide-runners get paid on Friday and bunk in the Hive all weekend, so the prospectors show up for the gambling. Rudder-rookies and swabbies, too. Put your money away." I pushed her hand toward the pouch on her belt. "You can't bribe some ooze-digger to take you down to the Saloon." Everything about her was asking for trouble, from her cavalier attitude to her long, loose hair.

"But I've shown Richard's picture everywhere else,"

she said, pushing her money back into the pouch. "The general store, library, computer lounge—"

"Okay. We'll hang out on the Access Deck. You can look over the prospectors as they dock their rigs and come aboard."

"But what about all the ones already in the Saloon?" She had that look I was beginning to recognize: jaw set, her mouth a firm line of determination.

"Listen," I said, trying another tact, "there's something I didn't tell you or anyone last night. After the house collapsed, I was out in the field alone. I saw Shade."

Gemma's eyes widened.

"He was so white he looked like a dead man." I paused, then admitted, "I followed him."

"Did you find their lair?"

I almost rolled my eyes at the drama she was laying on it. *Lair.* "No, he attacked me and took my manta-board." At her gasp, I went on. "I'm telling you because that's the kind of man who's in the Saloon." I pointed at the floor, indicating the level below us. "You're picturing your brother, but that's not what you're going to find."

"Were his eyes pink?"

"Shade's?"

She nodded. Her excitement reminded me of Zoe whenever Pa made up a story about a sea monster.

"He didn't even have eyes. Just gaping black holes."

Gemma clamped her hand to her mouth.

"That's what it looked like anyway. I'm sure he was just wearing dark contact lenses."

"Probably because his eyes are sensitive. I've read that a lot of albinos are nearly blind."

"He saw me well enough. He managed to shoot a harpoon right into my mantaboard."

She dropped her hand. "You're trying to scare me."

Just then the elevator doors opened and an unsteady miner sauntered out. Gemma backed away, only to bump into me, which caused her to stumble forward, right into the miner. "Sorry," she mumbled.

"No problem, pretty lady." The man's leer revealed his yellowing teeth.

When the man continued on his way, I turned to her. "See what I'm saying?"

She grinned and held up a green ID card. An adult ID card.

I couldn't believe it. "You picked that miner's pocket!"

Not even a tinge of guilt crossed her face. "My brother taught me that trick." She pushed the elevator call button.

"Stealing isn't a trick." I stepped between her and the elevator doors. "Listen to me. You'll be an angelfish swimming with eels down there."

"Eels don't scare me," she said as the doors slid open. She wasn't really going down to the Saloon. She was bluffing. I was sure of it. But then she stepped around me and into the elevator. "I'll tell you what it's like when I get back," she said with a wave.

I grabbed her by the hand and tugged her out before the doors closed. "If you're going to do it, at least be smart about it." I dragged her down the hall. "You can't go in as a girl."

"What am I supposed to go as? A jellyfish?"

I opened the door to a storage room. "A boy." I pulled clothes from a large bin. "It's the Trade Station's lost and found." I thrust a crumpled red sweatshirt at her.

She wrinkled her nose. "No way."

"Right. You're used to fancy dresses."

"All my dresses are hand-me-downs, but they don't stink like cigars and sweat."

"Dirty is a good thing considering the company you'll be keeping." I pushed the hooded sweatshirt into her hands. She made a pained face but pulled it over her head. I studied her as she smoothed the sweatshirt into place and tugged its hood down so that most of her hair was hidden from view. With her long bangs falling into her eyes, she might pass for a boy. Then I took in the whole picture and groaned. This wasn't going to work.

"Stop staring at my chest," she snapped.

"It's a problem."

"Excuse me?"

"We have to do something to hide it or else the men in the Saloon are going to go way past staring."

For the first time, Gemma looked uncertain.

"You find some baggy pants in there." I pointed at the clothes bin. "I'll be right back."

She stepped into my path. "Where're you going?"

"To get a bandage so you can flatten everything out." My worry had pushed me way past embarrassment. Her cheeks, however, blazed like a sunset over the ocean. "When we're in the Saloon, don't do that," I told her.

"Do what?"

"Blush. It makes you look like a girl." I headed for the infirmary.

"I *am* a girl!" she called.

As if I hadn't noticed.

CHAPTER

FOURTEEN

I hesitated in the doorway of the infirmary. Everything about this room sickened me—the smell, the spotless cabinets, and, most of all, the medical equipment. Just seeing the crash cart in my peripheral vision made my stomach flop like a hooked cod. Still, I forced myself inside.

"Doc, are you here?" I called out.

I tacked toward his office at the back where the door stood open, passing stacks of boxes along the way. I couldn't believe the 'wealth was recalling him. What if one of the settlers got seriously hurt? As much as I loathed the smells and sounds of an infirmary, if a shark tore up my leg, I'd still rather have Doc stitch it up than Raj or some other unqualified settler.

Doc wasn't in his office, which looked almost entirely packed up. As I turned to leave, I knocked into an open box and sent it toppling. I bent to pick up the scattered files, only to freeze when I recognized a title: "Dark Gifts: A Subsea Phenomenon" by Dr. William Metzger. It was the stupid article that Gemma kept asking about. I scanned the page, picking out: . . . *conducted brain scans on adolescents who have resided subsea for extended periods of time. The results reveal that they have more areas of active brain use . . . in theory, the intense water pressure stimulates the brain's development and results in abnormal abilities . . . many of these adolescents display traits associated with marine life.* I got to my feet, still clutching the page when Doc strode into the office. He didn't seem at all annoyed to see me standing amid his scattered files.

"Looking for me?" he asked.

"I need a bandage," I managed to croak. When he looked me over, I added, "Not for me. No one's hurt. I just need it."

"Okay," he said and pulled open a drawer.

I relaxed. He wasn't going to make me explain. "Why do you have this?" I asked, holding up the paper.

He tossed me the rolled bandage. "When I took this job, I downloaded every article I could find on the territory so I'd know what I was getting into."

"Did you believe everything you read?"

He grimaced. "I've been a government employee too long for that. I know better. The 'wealth has a whole department devoted to pushing its agenda on the public." He rubbed his scarred palm. "Or discrediting anyone who's viewed as a threat."

"Like the scientists who say the oceans have stopped rising."

"Exactly. If the Commonwealth isn't in the midst of a crisis, there's no reason to operate under Emergency Law. The state representatives aren't about to give up that kind of power."

I placed the article back in the box and bent to retrieve the rest. As Doc knelt to help me, he asked, "Does that article bother you?"

With a shrug, I turned for the door. "Thanks for the bandage."

"I entered a sample of the blood we found on the derelict sub into the main computer," Doc said.

Curious, I faced him again.

"If the man's DNA is in the government's data bank," Doc went on, "I'll know his name by tonight."

"So it *was* human blood?"

"Yes," Doc said grimly. "And whoever bled out in that sub won't be stopping by to collect his gear. No one could lose that much and live."

I winced. Why would the Seablite Gang murder a prospector? What could he have owned that they wanted so badly? "Thanks for the bandage," I said, turning to go.

Doc touched my shoulder. "I need to talk to you about your friend Gemma."

Feeling more than a little uncomfortable, I watched him cross to his desk.

"This was sent to me this morning." He rolled back his chair so that I could see what was on his screen: a photo of Gemma in a high-neck caftan, probably taken from an ID card. "It went to all the staff at the Trade Station. It's a missing child post, filed by a boarding home." He studied me. "It says that she stole money from the director's office."

My heart sank like an anchor. "Are you going to report her?"

He considered it. "No," he said finally. "But someone else might."

"Then Gemma and I don't have much time."

Doc raised a brow. "For what?"

"Thanks," I said, and sprinted for the door.

"It's *my* money! Richard sent it to me and Ms. Spinner took it," Gemma fumed. "She said she'd give it back when I wasn't her responsibility. But how is *that* going to happen unless Richard signs my emancipation form? I needed the money to get here."

"How *did* you get here?"

"Like I want another lecture." She plucked the bandage from my fingers and ducked back into the lost and found, leaving me to wait nervously in the corridor.

When she finally stepped out of the storage room, I said, "The hall is empty. Let's go."

"So I pass?"

"Yeah." If you looked closely, you'd still be able to tell she was a girl. But I didn't think the denizens of the Saloon ever looked at anyone too closely. Some lowlife might take offense. I checked around the corner and beckoned her over my shoulder. "If we're going into the Saloon, it's got to be now, while no one is here."

"Who's going to stop us?" she scoffed.

"Actually"—I called up another reinforcement of patience—"if a settler sees me, he'll not only stop me from going into the Saloon, he'll drag me home by the scruff of my diveskin."

"Why?" She seemed genuinely perplexed.

"These people are my neighbors. Down here, that means something. The Saloon is the one place in Benthic Territory where, hopefully, no one will recognize me. But who knows? Maybe our librarian is down there kicking back the booze."

"That's the nicest thing I've ever heard," she said softly.

"That our librarian drinks?"

She gave a choked laugh. "That everybody looks out for you."

"Yeah. It's nice until I do something I shouldn't and my parents hear about it from six sources. By the way, sneaking into the Saloon falls into that category. So if you've changed your—"

"Haven't." She gave me the once-over. "But if people are looking out for you, you should put on new clothes, too."

When the elevator doors opened on sublevel three, a tsunami of noise swept over us. I was dressed as a tidal mill roustabout in a blue jumpsuit and knit cap, which I pulled down to my eyes. I wasn't worried so much about the customers recognizing me, but in the ten years since the Trade Station was built, I'd met most of the staff. We stepped onto a catwalk four stories above the Saloon floor. Gemma gasped. "Why are we up here?"

"This is the Hive. You wanted to bunk here, remember?" I pointed to either side of the center shaft, where three levels of windowed hatches lined the walls, resembling a giant honeycomb. Still, Gemma hung back. "If you want to get to the Saloon, we have to take three stairladders down."

Although it had been years since I had been on this level, I knew the layout because I had free run of the place when my father supervised the Trade Station's construction. Back then, the Recreation Deck had felt serene with its four-story wall of windows and underwater view. The view remained, but the shouting and clanking tankards demolished all sense of serenity.

I crossed the top catwalk to peer over the railing at the Saloon far below. It was like looking down on an eel garden, except that every so often a burst of flame would erupt. Seaweed cigars needed continual relighting, so the tables had built-in burners. At the bar, men pushed against one another unsteadily. Still, I'd rub shoulders with gamblers and wildcatters over a wealthy Topsider any day. I glanced at Gemma, who was unusually pale.

"Having second thoughts?" I asked.

She glowered at me like a hermit crab defending its shell.

"Come on. You'll feel right at home," I teased. "With all the people and noise, it could be the mainland." She backed deeper into the elevator alcove. "What's wrong?"

Grimacing, she pointed at the catwalk. The steel mesh was so fine that even though there were two more catwalks beneath it, I could still see the Saloon floor. With its suspension wires and thin railings, the whole structure did seem like temporary scaffolding.

"You'll be the lightest person to ever walk on it." I stamped my foot. Sure, the catwalk trembled, but that was a good thing. Every part of the Trade Station was designed to give a little. Or sometimes, a lot. The Surface Deck would automatically disengage from the lower station if any of the lower levels sprang a leak. Somehow, I didn't think Gemma would find comfort in that fact.

"Look, it's perfectly safe," I said, throwing my weight from side to side so that all three levels swayed. Again, that was a good thing in subsea architecture, but Gemma remained backed against the elevator doors.

"I thought you were desperate to find your brother."

She started coming forward again.

"Shoot," I muttered. I'd just blown my chance to get her out of here, all because I wanted her to see that my father's design was safe. I bounced on the balls of my feet, making the catwalk jump. "Actually, this does feel flimsy."

"Walk away," she snapped. "Now."

I shrugged. Leaning against a suspension wire, I watched her leave the alcove and pick her way along the row of sleeping capsules.

Footsteps clanged beneath us and a voice bellowed, "Get away from my berth!"

Spreading my feet, I looked down to see two men on the catwalk below. I recognized Lefty Hathaway, the proprietor of the Hive.

"It's not your berth no more," Lefty growled at the man facing him.

Other than collecting the nightly fee, Lefty didn't have to do much except keep the berths clean. The Hive was the ultimate efficiency hotel, in which the "rooms" weren't much bigger than coffins. Prospectors rented them by the night, while mining companies contracted for whole rows and the miners lived in the cramped capsules all year long.

Below, the fight about the prospector's nonpayment escalated. Gemma's breathing quickened as she peered down at the two men, who were now throwing punches. Their efforts had all three catwalks jumping and she swallowed hard like she was about to puke.

"They're just eels. They don't scare you, remember?" I reminded her.

"Those aren't eels," she said. "Those are psychos."

When Lefty whipped out a jagged blade, the prospector pounded up the stairladder.

"Psychos with big knives," Gemma amended. "They're going to make this stupid thing fall down."

"Probably," I agreed cheerfully. "Can we leave now?"

"No!" She pulled her hood down to her eyes. "I didn't come subsea to get scared away by a couple of—" She screamed as the prospector flew past us—thrown by Lefty, who was now at the top of the stairs. She caught my look of warning.

"Boys scream," she whispered defensively.

"So do men. If we stick around, I'm sure we'll hear one."

"Scaring me isn't going to work." She headed for the stairladder.

Lefty blocked her way, squinting with suspicion. "You're too young to be on this level."

"Our ma sent us," she said in a husky voice. "We're supposed to find our pa and bring him home."

To my surprise, Lefty nodded. "Okay." He let her pass. "Just be quick."

Pulling my cap low, I followed Gemma down the stairladder to the middle catwalk. "Good act," I admitted grudgingly. "You sounded like a real pioneer."

She grinned. "I was doing you."

"Me?"

"Some people have poker faces, you have a poker voice. Guarded and a little hoarse. I nailed it." The clang of boots on the second stairladder ended her boasting.

I beckoned her away from the top of the ladder. "You can't go down if someone's coming up. There isn't room." I didn't sound guarded or hoarse.

She peeked over the railing and inhaled sharply. "It's your friend. Jibby."

"Is he alone?"

"There's a man behind him. Big guy. Bushy black beard."

That had to be Raj, whose mouth was even bigger than his ego. They'd see through my disguise in a click. Whirling, I pried open an empty capsule and motioned to Gemma, who gamely climbed inside. I wiggled in after her and closed the hatch.

At five, I'd loved the cozy berths complete with shelves, a fold-down desk, and a computer screen—all built into the walls. But the capsules were designed to hold one person, and seemed much smaller now that I wasn't five. As we lay on our stomachs, it was a very snug fit.

Through the tinted window in the hatch, I saw Jibby climb onto the catwalk. "Ranger Grimes is going to turn the derelict sub over to the Seaguard," he said, passing right by our berth.

Sure enough, Raj Dirani clambered up next, bigger and louder than life. "Grimes doesn't give a barnacle's knee if a prospector gets killed. He won't go after the scum that did it."

With one boot on the stairladder, Jibby paused to listen to him. I'd made the right choice by hiding. Raj took parental duty very seriously. Probably because he was raising his twelve-year-old daughter alone. He would've hauled me back to Ma and Pa without breaking stride.

Inside the berth, Gemma sat back on her knees. The top of her head cleared the ceiling by inches. "Glacial," she whispered. "I wish I had this much space of my own." She leaned across me and pried open a door in the capsule wall, then ooohed with delight over the minifridge.

"Shhh. These aren't sound—" I choked on my words when Raj smacked a hand to the hatch window and leaned against it.

"The Seablite Gang sunk the Peaveys' house," Raj went on. "It's a fact. We let it go by and those outlaws will think they can help themselves to anything that's ours. Crops . . . livestock . . . I can't get a woman to come subsea on account of them!"

"Ever think it might be on account of your smell?" I heard Jibby ask.

Raj snorted and headed for the last stairladder.

Once their boots were out of sight, I flipped onto my back, to find Gemma leaning over me. She pressed a hand to my chest for balance as she switched on the screen above the hatch. "Oh, it's a phone, too." She sat back, smiling. "We have everything we need in here. We could hide out for days and see who goes by. Hey, you're glowing again." She considered me a moment. "I think you glow more when you're embarrassed. Maybe that's how you blush."

"I'm not embarrassed." Now I sounded hoarse. Total poker voice. I pushed open the hatch and climbed out. Spending days inside a berth with her was too unsettling to think about given our precarious situation. I needed to focus. Looking up through the steel mesh catwalk, I watched Jibby and Raj disappear into the elevator. "And I don't glow."

"Please," she scoffed, climbing out of the berth. "Fireflies have nothing on you."

Rather than ask what a firefly was, I said, "Before we hit the Saloon, we need a plan."

"Like what?"

"Like don't go up to anyone. Just look for your brother in the crowd . . . but don't make eye contact."

"Aye aye, Captain."

I followed her down the next two stairladders, whispering more instructions as they came to me. "And don't flash his photo around. You don't know if he's on someone's bad side."

"Got it," she said over her shoulder as she alighted onto the Saloon floor.

Staggering drunks surrounded us, but that didn't faze Gemma. She cut her way through the mob, easy as you please, leaving me to trail in her wake. At least she was following the plan, I thought . . . until she clapped a slim blond man on the shoulder. When he turned, she thrust her brother's picture at him. Maybe if she'd waited to get a good look at the guy's ice blue eyes, she wouldn't have been so quick to demand, "Have you seen him?"

At most, the guy had three years on us. More likely, he had two and a fake ID. Yet there was nothing young about his hard expression. His hair was dead straight, almost white, and so long that it touched his ribs. He glanced at the photo. For a split second, I saw surprise flash across his face, but when he lifted his gaze, I wondered if I was wrong. Friendly as a barracuda, he stared at Gemma. Studying her, I realized with a start. Taking in every detail of her face.

I plucked the photo from her fingers. "Either you've seen him or not," I said, stepping in.

"Not," he replied coldly, then slipped away through the crowd.

"Will you please stop drawing attention to yourself?" I whispered angrily.

For some reason, that had Gemma snorting with laughter. I clapped my hand over her mouth with striking speed as men turned on their stools to look over.

"Okay, here's the deal," I said in my bossiest big brother voice. "You don't talk while we're in here because even when you're doing me, you sound like a girl. Same as when you laugh. And don't poke any more strangers." She shoved my hand away. "I mean it. Or I'll drag you straight to the ranger and tell him you're a runaway and wanted for stealing."

Now her eyes were alight with fury.

"Are we clear?"

She said nothing, just steamed.

"Gemma?"

"You told me not to talk," she hissed.

"What are you boys doing in here?" a voice behind us demanded.

I spun in time to see the bartender slam the counter open and storm over to us. The man was old and missing an eye. "I'm not losing my license over a pair of guppies like you."

Before I could reply, a second bartender leaned over the counter. "Leave them alone, Otto." The pitch of the voice told me that a woman was addressing us. Still, it was hard to reconcile that with the narrow-eyed, shaved-head bartender in front of us. "Boys, you better tack out of here if you know what's good for you," she said.

Gemma snatched Richard's photo from my hand. "We don't mean to cause you trouble, mister," she said, doing another lousy imitation of me, but even gruffer this time. She offered the photo to the bartender named Otto. "We're just here to look for my brother. He doesn't know that our ma is sick. Have you seen him?"

The man's expression softened.

"Now you feel like crap, don't you, Otto?" the female bartender taunted. "Next time ask a few questions before worrying about your license."

"Shut up, Mel." The old man took the photo from Gemma and squinted his one eye at it. "Nope. I don't believe I've seen him." He passed the photo to Mel.

She shook her head, too. "Not that I remember every ugly mug that comes down here," she added, handing the photo back to me. "But I try to keep an eye on the young ones. You never know what will happen in this cesspool."

"Why don't you leave the picture with us," Otto suggested. "We'll show it to these thugs when they buy drinks. It's not safe for you boys to stick around down here."

I was in total agreement but before I could convince Gemma of anything, I noticed the icy blond guy in a back corner, whispering into the ear of a huge dark-skinned man.

"Let's get out of here." I pressed a hand to Gemma's back. "Now." But it was too late. The big man's eyes were on us.

"We just got here," she whispered, not budging under the pressure of my hand. "We'll pretend to leave and then mix in with the crowd."

I couldn't peel my eyes off the leviathan seated on the other side of the Saloon. He had his back to the glass wall, which had to be on purpose. His skin was so dark he practically disappeared against the murky blue sea outside. He wore pants and a sharkskin vest but no shirt. Showing off his chest, which was roped with muscle. His face was unreadable, as if it had been carved from granite. His features were broad and heavy. His head clean-shaven and—

Recognition hit me like a crowbar to the gut.

I knew the shape of that skull. The slash of that mouth. So what if the man's skin was now brown, not stark white? There was no doubt in my mind. None at all.

It was Shade.

CHAPTER

FIFTEEN

"Shade," I hissed, tugging at Gemma's arm. "He's over there."

She squinted in the direction I was looking. "How can you see anything in—" Her words were lost on a sharp intake of air. I didn't blame her; the size of the man would scare anyone. And worse, he was staring right at her. Lifting her chin in defiance, she glared back at him. Quick as an eel, I slipped in front of her to block the outlaw's view. This was not the time for Gemma to prove how tough she was.

"You said he was an albino," she whispered, trying to peer around me.

"He was." I shuffled her backward. "Maybe he covers himself in zinc-paste when he's robbing supply ships. I don't know. But that's him." I steered her toward the stairladder. "Listen, you've got to get Ranger Grimes. He'll be in the Observatory. Tell him to come down right away and you stay up there."

Torn, she glanced over my shoulder at Shade. "What are you going to do?"

"Wait here so I can point him out to Grimes." I wondered if I'd have to shove her up every step.

"But—"

"I'll meet you in the Observatory after the ranger arrests him." Saying it out loud gave me hope. Who'd have guessed that sneaking into the Saloon was the best move I could have made to help the territory? Not that Ma and Pa would view it that way.

"The ranger is going to want to know who I am," Gemma protested. "What am I supposed to say?"

"You'll come up with something." After seeing her in action, I didn't doubt it for a second.

Frowning, she darted up the stairladder. I turned to see Shade get to his feet. Looking bored and intent at the same time, the outlaw peeled off his sharkskin vest and tossed it to another man, not the one with the ice blue eyes. This guy had a wide grin and dark hair swept back with a bandanna. No doubt another member of the Seablite Gang.

Shade strolled out from under the catwalk to watch Gemma inching along overhead. Warning bells clanged in my mind, sending vibrations to my fingertips. I sprang forward. No way was I going to let this opportunity slip away. Scary as he was, I had to distract Shade until the ranger got here, hopefully with backup.

Shade saw me coming, as did the guys flanking him. I knuckled down my jitters and kept walking. I needed an excuse for approaching them, and quick. Ten feet from the outlaws, I took out the photo of Gemma's brother. I had my excuse, but still I stumbled to a stop upon getting a better look at Shade. Up close, he wasn't as dark skinned as I'd thought. Black tattoos swirled over his bare chest, spiraled up his muscled arms and wrapped around his neck and skull like the tentacles of a squid. No wonder he covered his face with zinc.

Suddenly a drunk pushed into me and knocked the photo from my hand. I dove for it, landing in the mixture of spit, alcohol, and mud from a hundred soles that slicked the Saloon floor. As my fingers touched the photo, a booted foot stomped onto my hand. My fingers throbbed with pain. A second later the foot lifted. At least the photo was laminated. As I wiped it off on my diveskin, I stood up, expecting to face Shade. . . .

But he wasn't there.

Instead, his bandanna-wearing henchman thumped his booted feet onto the table. He grinned at me, revealing two gold teeth among his pearly whites. The other outlaw with the icy stare now lounged in the chair that Shade had vacated. My skin prickled.

Turning in place, I scanned the raucous crowd around me. There was no way Shade had time to make it across the Saloon to the stairs. I pushed through the swaying bodies to check the card tables that ran along the far wall. He could have mingled in with the gamblers, yet I saw no dark, bald head among them and Shade didn't seem like a man who would crouch under a table. But there was nowhere else to hide. The exterior wall was one big bank of windows, looking out onto a twilight sea. The Hive started at the first catwalk, so he couldn't have crawled into a berth without first climbing the stairs.

"Looking for someone?" asked the dark-haired outlaw. He had the carefree attitude of a floater.

"Yes." I closed the distance between us. These two might be in Shade's gang but they weren't escaped convicts. Both were too young to have been in prison five years ago. They looked barely old enough to be in the Saloon at all.

I flashed the photo at the blue-eyed outlaw. "You recognize him, don't you?" I asked with more confidence than I felt. "I saw it in your face at the bar."

He didn't betray so much as a twitch, just continued to stare at me coldly.

"Leave off, Pretty," admonished the other outlaw. "You're scaring the child."

"I already said no." Pretty's voice was low and lethal.

"Pretty?" I stammered.

"Ain't he just? But only on the outside." The dark-haired man's eyes gleamed with amusement. "I'm Eel."

"Not your real name," I said stupidly.

He smirked. "Wouldn't want to complicate things."

The gas burner in the center of the table sent up a flame, jarring me. Even more startling: The firelight brought out the glimmer in Eel's skin.

"You have a shine!"

"You're one to talk," he said with a laugh.

It didn't make sense. To build up a visible shine—even one as faint as Eel's—took years of eating abyssal fish. Only people who lived on the ocean floor had easy access to those fish. I swung my attention to Pretty. Sure enough, now that I was looking for it, I saw the telltale shimmer in his pale skin. Yet the Seablite Gang had shown up less than a year ago.

"When did you live subsea? And where?" Benthic Territory was the only underwater settlement in the world and I knew that Eel and Pretty, under any names, had never been fellow pioneers.

A knife flashed in Pretty's hand. Before I could react, Eel plucked the photo from my fingers. "Hey!"

"Who's this?" he asked, studying the picture.

Keeping Pretty's blade in view, I said, "I don't know." Eel raised a skeptical brow. "I don't," I insisted. "Some Topside girl posted it online. Says he's a prospector in Benthic Territory. She's offering a chunk of money to anyone who finds him." They exchanged a look that I couldn't interpret. I held my hand out for the photo. "If you can't help me—"

"Where'd the other boy go?" Pretty asked.

He meant Gemma. "Nowhere. He got jumpy, so he left."

Eel leaned back in his chair, seemingly nonchalant. "To fetch the ranger?"

I wasn't fooled. His question was as serious as the knife in Pretty's hand. Again, I played stupid. "Why would he do that?"

Eel's gaze shifted past me. "No reason at all." He flipped me the photo.

"I know you're not giving this young'un trouble," a familiar voice warned. I turned to find Mel behind me, wielding a shock-rifle, with its double prongs aimed at Eel's head.

"He came over to us." Eel put up his hands in mock surrender.

Mel waved me forward with the tip of the rifle. "And now he's leaving you."

"Thanks," I whispered as I slipped past her.

"See you when you're eighteen," she replied.

"If he lives that long," I heard Pretty hiss. Without looking back, I sprinted for the stairladder.

"Then poof, he was gone?" the ranger scoffed, without taking his eye from one of the many telescopes set up around the Observatory.

Here was the ranger's chance to arrest Shade, yet Grimes seemed like he couldn't care less.

"You have to believe me," I fumed. I was risking the outlaws' wrath by talking to the ranger, as well as guaranteeing that my parents would hear about me sneaking into the Saloon. Still, I had to convince Grimes to use the information. "We were face-to-face yesterday on the Peaveys' property. The man in the Saloon is Shade."

The Observatory was walled with glass. Only the elevator shaft in the center of the trapezoidal room kept the view from being nonstop ocean and horizon. I had ditched the roustabout jumpsuit but Gemma was still wearing the dirty red sweatshirt and baggy pants. She sat calmly enough on the bench that bounded the entire space and kept her face hidden inside her hood. Still, I could tell that she was itching to leave the ranger's office.

Straightening, Ranger Grimes glared at me. "What were you and your *cousin* even doing on the Rec Deck? Don't try to tell me either one o' you is eighteen."

It took me a second to realize he meant Gemma. I knew she'd come up with something. "It's his first visit," I said. "I wanted to show him—"

"How to waste a government official's time?" Grimes asked with a derisive snort. "There ain't but one way out of the Saloon, boy, and that's up the stairs. So where'd your outlaw go?"

"I told you, I don't know." I gritted my teeth. Another adult treating me like a kid.

"And aside from that, the man is albino," Grimes said in a patronizing tone. "Everyone he's ever robbed says so."

"He must smear his face with zinc-paste," I guessed. "So he can drink in the Saloon and no one will recognize him."

"You did. Or so you say."

"By the shape of his face."

Ranger Grimes shot me a dubious look.

"Sometimes," I explained haltingly, "I don't see things in color."

"You're color-blind . . . *sometimes*?"

"Yeah. So, I focus on the contours of an object." I stole another glance at Gemma, but she didn't seem to be paying attention. She was too busy patting the glass wall as if to assure herself that it was impossible to fall onto the Surface Deck several stories below. "Look, I know for a fact he's Shade," I told Grimes. "Will you at least go down to the lower station and look for him?"

"You people give me the bends."

Gemma's hand froze midpat. "What people?" she asked gruffly.

"Not you. The Dark Life." Grimes pointed at me. "They're all oxygen deprived. Especially the kids."

"They don't like to be called Dark Life." Her chin tilted mutinously.

"How long have you been here visiting? A day? Stick around, you'll see. Living in the dark makes them crazy. Makes them see things that aren't there."

"Ty doesn't live in the dark."

"He sure don't live in the sunshine." Ranger Grimes faced me. "What's the longest you ever been Topside, boy? A whole day? Not even. A supply run takes six hours round-trip."

"I lived Topside for four months."

The ranger sauntered over to Gemma. "It's the water pressure, you know." He pressed his hand on the top of her head. "Pushing down on them all the time. It scrambles their brains."

She ducked from under his palm. "You live down here."

"Thank you for your time, Ranger Grimes." I waved her toward the elevator.

"I live here," the ranger corrected, pointing upward to indicate his rooms on the floor above. "And I don't swim around on the ocean floor. If we was supposed to fill up our lungs with liquid, God would have made us fish."

Scowling, Gemma joined me by the elevator.

"I'll fetch the sub," I said, pressing the call button, "while you get your things." She said nothing, just shot the ranger a dirty look over her shoulder. "You know how to get to the lounge, right?" I tugged open the stairwell door, next to the elevator. "It's inside the Surface Deck. You have to take the stairs down—"

"I know where the lockers are."

I let the stairwell door swing shut. "Something wrong?"

"Why'd you let him talk to you like that?" she demanded.

I glanced back to see if Grimes was listening, but no, he'd settled behind his desk and popped open a pill bottle as if we'd already left. "He's just mad he got stationed out here."

"That means he can treat you like crap? Why didn't you stick up for yourself?"

"He's a ranger." I wished she'd lower her voice. "What was I supposed to say?"

"Tell him to shut his ignorant mouth."

"Right. And give him a reason to think that settlers aren't only crazy but rude." The elevator arrived with a ding.

She hauled open the stairwell door. "Don't you ever get sick of being so good?"

I flushed. "I'm not so good!" Not even close. But she slipped into the stairwell and banged the door closed behind her.

"Is there a problem with that elevator, boy?" the ranger shouted from his desk.

Without replying, I stepped into the transparent cylinder and hit the button for the Access Deck. As the doors closed, I slumped against the center column and inhaled deeply. The elevator dropped out of the tower, speeding down the cable, past the inner docking-ring. I looked for Gemma on the suspended footbridges but didn't see her before the elevator plunged beneath the ocean's surface.

"I figured you for dead," said a low rumble of a voice.

My heart sat up in my chest.

I whirled to find Shade, leaning against the elevator's transparent wall, his dark eyes gleaming like a shark's. The center column had hidden him from view.

"I left you in the deep sea." Shade's voice was rich. Hypnotic. "Without a vehicle, without a weapon." His thickly muscled arms were crossed over his bare chest. "How come you're still alive?"

CHAPTER

SIXTEEN

Water surrounded the elevator, giving the interior an eerie glow. Frozen in place, I registered every detail of the outlaw. The pockmarked skin. The black tattoos that covered Shade's head, neck, and shoulders like tentacles. And his perfectly normal, dark brown eyes. No wonder he wore black contact lenses when he was trying to pass for albino.

I backed away. "I don't know what you're—"

"Don't ink me." He punched a knuckle onto the EMERGENCY STOP button. The elevator jerked to a halt halfway down the cable. "I know when I've been made."

His anger was no more than a flash but it was enough to terrify me into dropping all pretenses. "What do you want?"

"Let's start with what you told the ranger."

"About?" I slid my fingers toward my knife holster, refusing to panic.

"You've seen the real me. That's got to be worth a pat on the head." The outlaw stepped forward. "Considering that Grimes has been swimming in circles for over a year, searching for an albino." Dropping his gaze, Shade burned my hand with his stare.

"I told him you're dark skinned." I straightened, leaving my knife in its holster. Only then did Shade raise his gaze. "But he didn't believe me."

"That so?" Shade drawled.

I tried to cop Eel's nonchalant attitude in the Saloon. "Ranger Grimes hates all settlers. Thinks we're crazy and stupid for living subsea." I could swear that the outlaw's tattoos were now moving, sliding over his arms, writhing like sea snakes. "He kicked me out of his office for wasting his time." I blinked and Shade's tattoos were back in place.

"You didn't answer me," Shade chided.

"Yes, I—"

"Anyone else would have gotten lost in the open ocean. Eaten. But not you. Why?"

"Luck," I said.

A ghost of a smile floated over his lips. "Some might call it a gift." He studied me for a moment. "A Dark Gift."

"There's no such thing," I said stiffly. "Dark Gifts are a myth."

White teeth gleamed in the shadows as he circled the column.

"I should know," I went on, following him with my eyes. "If any kid would have one, it would be me. I was born subsea."

"Now that's interesting. . . ."

As I twisted to keep him in sight, Shade grabbed me by the back of the neck. "Here I was planning on choking the life out of you." His tone was as harsh as his hold. "To keep you quiet . . . forever."

I felt my pulse throbbing under his fingertips.

"But you're born-and-bred Dark Life," he went on, "and that's something." His fingers bit into my flesh. "Don't you ever"—his grip tightened—"let anyone tell you different. Especially not some government stooge." He released me and knuckled the emergency button again.

As the elevator resumed its descent, I clenched my teeth to hold in a cough. I wouldn't give him that satisfaction.

Smirking, Shade eyed me as if he knew exactly what I was doing. "Kid, I'm giving you one chance. One." The elevator doors slid open. "Talk about me again—I will kill you."

With that, he stepped out of the elevator and disappeared into the shadows.

CHAPTER

SEVENTEEN

Still shaken from my encounter with Shade, I zoomed the Slicky to the surface and crashed through the waves. Why had he let me go? Why hadn't he killed me?

It wasn't mercy.

No, it was something else. But I wasn't sure what.

When the spray settled around the egg-shaped minisub, I saw Gemma standing on the docking-ring with a large duffel bag by her feet. Her back to me, she stomped out of the stained, baggy pants and kicked them through an open door, into the visitors' lounge.

I steered the Slicky into a vacant slip several hitching posts down from her and popped the hatch. Though it was only midafternoon, the sky was as dark as dusk, which was more than fine with me. I tipped my face toward the gray clouds and welcomed the feel of rain on my skin. Water in any form cleared my mind. Even the throb in my neck where Shade had gripped me dulled.

There was no fish market on the weekends, so the Surface Deck was nearly deserted—exactly how I liked it. Only a couple of fishermen fought their way through the downpour.

As I stood on the seat, a chill slid over me. Not a stiff breeze, but a sense of alarm. Why? I scanned the Surface Deck. Something was wrong with the view, though exactly what, I couldn't tell.

"Gemma!" I yelled. "Over—" The words shriveled in my throat as movement caught my eye. On the promenade, a dark form glided against the backdrop of gray sky. Its outline was human, but the figure was featureless. A shadow, yet there was no sun out, or man nearby to cast it.

"Ty!" She waved, oblivious to the patch of night that grew larger as it neared the railing above her. Scooping up her duffel, she sprinted down the docking-ring toward me. The shadow halted. When it raised its head to watch her go, I gasped. Twin red embers blazed where its eyes should have been . . . and then the embers were extinguished, and the shadow disappeared.

"Are you really going to tell the other settlers that Shade isn't an albino?" Gemma asked after I'd filled her in. It was fifteen minutes since the strange shadow had passed. The Slicky dropped through the sunlit water toward the dark blue of the deep.

"As soon as we get home."

"But Shade said he'd kill you!"

"I don't care what he said. I don't obey outlaws. Or keep their secrets." I leveled off the minisub at a depth of seventy feet, where only the brightest rays of sunlight pierced the water, but we weren't likely to run into any divers or fishing nets.

"But what if he comes after you?"

"I hope he does. There are over two hundred homesteads down here. If Shade searches every one, looking for me, someone is bound to harpoon him."

"He might wait for you to show up at the Trade Station again."

That thought tightened my gut. "Maybe. But if the settlers know he isn't albino, maybe we can catch him. With Shade in jail, Benthic Territory will have a chance."

"You mean your parents will stay and you'll be able to stake a claim in three years."

"Two and a half. Yeah. That's what I'm hoping," I admitted.

"Well, I hope he gets eaten by a killer whale."

"Orcas don't eat people." Steering with one hand, I unzipped the pouch on my belt. "I still have your brother's photo." As I offered it to her, I realized that my impression of the skinny, freckled boy had changed. Yesterday, I'd only noticed that her brother shared her russet hair and blue eyes. Now, I saw the twinkle in Richard's eyes and that his smile was genuine and warm.

Of course, now I knew that he'd jeopardized his freedom to make sure that his little sister didn't feel abandoned.

"It would be easier if he was more distinctive looking," Gemma said, taking the photo. "Like you."

Her words packed the pain of a sucker punch. "I'm not distinctive looking."

Her lips twitched.

"Except for my shine, I look totally normal." I knew I sounded defensive but I couldn't help it. Gemma snickered and heat flashed through me. "Are you laughing at me?"

"Yes," she said emphatically. "You think those women yesterday wanted to touch you just because of your skin?"

"They'd never seen a shine before. It happens all the time." Why did she insist on talking about things I'd just as soon forget?

"You're so stupid," she said, barely containing her amusement. "If we were on the mainland, girls would break my arm to stand next to you."

"If you're trying to say they'd like me, you're wrong. Mainland girls visit the Trade Station. Not often, but if I come along when they're there, know what happens? They stop doing whatever they're doing and stare."

"I bet."

"Not like that. They stare like I belong in a floating sideshow." Kind of like the look she was giving me now.

After a moment, she said, "You know, you're right. Except for your shine, you're not distinctive at all." A smile hovered on her lips. "And if a girl stares at you, pay no attention to her."

I relaxed. "I'm not *that* thin-skinned."

"No, really. Ignore her completely." Gemma was pleased as could be about something, but who knew what. Her words were like silt, clouding the water.

Looking back to her brother's photo, she made a fist and then pressed it to her chest.

"What was that?"

"Just something we used to do across the air shaft," she replied. "Richard would stand at the window in the boys' dorm before lights-out and wait for me." She held up her fist. "This meant 'stay tough' and this"—she touched her fist to her heart—"meant he loved me."

I turned back to the control console and checked our position to avoid talking in case my voice came out choked. No wonder being tough was so important to her. Did Zoe care so much about what I thought of her? I seriously doubted it. But then, I wasn't her only living relative.

"What are you looking at?" Gemma asked.

Happy to change the subject, I told her. "Everything around and below us." I ran my finger over the continuously shifting graphic of the ocean floor, then straightened with realization. "You know what? We're near the building that Doc said was Seablite Prison."

"Really? Let's go—What's that?" She leaned across me to tap a corner of the screen.

The metallic fabric of my diveskin kept me from feeling the warmth of her arm stretched across my chest, but I imagined I could.

"There it is." She pointed out the window.

I followed her gesture and saw something huge and dark off to the right. Suddenly it dropped back. I cursed under my breath. I'd let myself get so distracted by her, I hadn't paid attention to the monitor. I zoomed the minisub upward and a shape popped onto the sonar screen. My mouth grew dry.

"Is it a whale?" she asked, leaning into me for a better look at the monitor.

As quickly as it appeared, the thing shot up and off the screen again. I looked up through the cockpit's glass cover. "Whales don't avoid sonar readings." I tried to stay calm.

"You think it's staying off our monitor on purpose?"

"Yeah." I needed a plan, quick. Even if I sent out a distress signal, no one would be able to get to us in time.

"Is it a sub?"

Only one submarine had that shape. I took a breath. "It's the *Specter.* Shade must have followed us from the Trade Station."

"Speed up!"

"We can't outrun—" The beating of a hundred pebbles hitting the roof cut off my words.

"What was that?"

"A net." I nodded at the viewport, which was covered with titanium mesh. Impossible to cut through. I shoved the joystick forward, causing the Slicky's nose to dip, trying to duck under the net's weighted edge. But it had already drawn closed around us. We were caught like halibut. All that was left to do was haul us in.

Looking up through the hatch, I saw the *Specter* high above us in the blue water. A circle of light appeared on the bottom of the outlaws' sub as the cover of the port slid back. A tough layer of clear plastic covered the opening, with an X sliced into its center. The outlaws would draw up their catch, positioning the Slicky right under the opening, until the hatch pushed through the center slit. I clamped the hatch lock, even though I knew that would only slow them down, not stop them from prying open the Slicky's cockpit like a clamshell.

"But Shade said he was giving you one chance," Gemma said.

I wrestled with the joystick, putting the sub into a hard reverse. The engine screamed in reaction.

"Can you believe it?" I said. "Shade lied."

"You don't have to be sarcastic."

"Sorry. I'm not used to being hunted by an outlaw."

The *Specter* sped forward, dragging us along. I banged the control panel. The Slicky's engine was no match against the *Specter*'s. Giving up, I cut the motor. Instantly the minisub jerked upward. "No way am I letting Shade haul us in."

"Ty, he *is* hauling us in."

"No, he's taking up the sub." I switched on the Slicky's heartbeat—a low mechanical pulse that would lead me to her later. "But we won't be inside. We're going to jump ship."

Her mouth spilled open.

"At this speed, by the time they get the Slicky into position and crack the hatch, they'll have crossed a mile at least. Shade won't know where to start looking for us."

"There could be sharks out there!"

"You'd rather be kidnapped by outlaws?" I thrust her helmet into her hands.

"Versus being eaten alive? Hmm, hard choice."

"Now who's being sarcastic?"

She glared at me like it was my fault that we were caught in a net. I was tempted to point out that she was the one who'd insisted on going into the Saloon. "We'll swim to the Peaveys'."

"I'm not leaving this sub."

"A lot of the settlers are there."

"I can't swim."

I paused, taken aback. "You came subsea and you don't know how to swim?"

"Don't make a big deal of it."

"Okay, listen," I said, trying to sound reassuring. "You don't have to swim. We're going to fall. You can fall, can't you?"

"A shark doesn't care if you're swimming or—"

"If there are any sharks around, I'll draw my shock-prod. I promise. We've got to go *now*."

She didn't budge. "No way. You can't see a shark this deep until it's already bitten off your head."

"If a predator is coming our way, I'll know."

"How?"

There was no other way. I had to tell her. I had to trust her. "I have a Dark Gift," I said, though I didn't look at her. I focused on snapping my helmet into place.

I have a Dark Gift. Did I really just admit it out loud?

"You said there's no such thing," she accused.

"I lied. Because I'm not always 'so good.' Put your helmet on."

CHAPTER

EIGHTEEN

Gemma froze with surprise or maybe disbelief; I couldn't tell. Plucking her helmet from her hands, I dropped it over her head. "I can see with sound," I explained, sealing her helmet. "It's called biosonar."

"You're Akai!"

"Yeah," I admitted. "That's the name the doctors put on my file. It means 'sea born.' Can we go now?" I pulled a lever on the side of my seat so that the back flipped down.

"How far does it work?"

I pulled the lever on her seat and sent her sprawling as her chair flattened. "A mile at least." I crawled to the exit port and shoved my feet through the ring. Luckily the net didn't wrap all the way across the Slicky's underside. "I'm going to hang on to the edge outside. Suck in Liquigen, then follow me as fast as you can."

"Wait!"

I didn't know if it was because she had more questions about my Dark Gift or because she was still afraid to jump, but I didn't stop to find out. I filled my lungs with

Liquigen and pushed through the rubber ring, catching hold of the edge of the port as I dropped out. My body whipped against the bottom of the Slicky, thrown by the *Specter*'s speed. Thankfully, Gemma's feet emerged instantly. As she slipped out, I hooked an arm around her waist and then let go of the ring's edge. Together, we dropped through the midnight-hued water.

Gemma turned in my arms to face me, slipped her hands around my waist, and hugged me so tightly our helmets banged together. Behind the acrylic glass, her eyes were scrunched closed.

High above us, the *Specter* zoomed past, still dragging the minisub. Good. The outlaws hadn't seen us exit. We'd be fine and so would the Slicky, I told myself. Most likely the outlaws would cut her loose when they found her cockpit empty. Then I'd hunt her down later.

Gemma opened her eyes as the sea darkened around us. We floated down through a cyclone of mackerel, flashing silver in the dim sunlight. As a sailfish cut past us, electric blue stripes appeared on its sides to confuse the mackerel. I felt Gemma's arms tighten around me. I met her eyes, expecting to see fear in her expression. But surprisingly, she was smiling as she took in the beauty of the wildlife swimming past.

She flipped on her crown lights. I did the same but the light only gave us about twenty feet of visibility. I cast out a web of sound to see what was below. The clicks I made in the back of my throat were too high pitched for Gemma to hear. I'd perfected them over the years, finding the sound that bounced back the quickest and was the easiest to interpret. Then my mind created an image out of the echoes I heard—like the sonar screen in the sub, with the peaks and valleys of the ocean floor sketched out in 3-D.

Using sign language, I told her to press the button that made fins slide out of the tips of her boots. Seeing her confusion, I chalked it up to another difference between growing up Topside versus subsea. Down here, we learned to sign before learning to talk. But then, we had to communicate with Liquigen-filled lungs. I pushed the control on her wrist screen for her, though even with fins, she didn't seem to get that she had to move her legs to stay level.

The computers in our diveskins automatically tinted our helmets for ultraviolet viewing, and the landscape beneath us jumped into sharp relief. We touched down in the middle of an enormous cloud of pink jellyfish. A thousand at least. All no bigger than my fist. Gently, I brushed them aside, cutting a path.

A siphonophore spun toward us, looking like twenty feet of glowing fishing net hung with silver bells. Gemma recoiled into me. Guessing that she'd never seen one before, I caught her hand and led her closer to the siphonophore. Then I tapped it to make it curl and undulate, knowing my dive glove would protect me from its stinging tentacles. With a quick stroke, I broke off a part. It wasn't one animal but hundreds all strung together. I bounced the broken-off part on my palm and then sent the shimmering piece over to Gemma. Her eyes were wide with wonder. As she cupped her hands around it, its soft yellow light made her skin glow.

I tipped my head to indicate that we should move on, but she couldn't take her eyes from the creature. If a siphonophore rocked her world, wait till she spent some real time down here. Suddenly I wanted to show her all the amazing places I'd found. And creatures. I wanted to see her face light up like that again.

Finally we began our trek toward the Peaveys' homestead. I'd driven over this area many times in a sub, but never trudged along the seafloor. Every moment or so, I clicked rapidly and waited for the echoes to bounce back to me. No large predators moved in the distance. I saw only dolphins, at least a hundred, swimming, leaping, and feeding near the ocean's surface. I could also feel their clicks and long drawn-out echoes falling around us, though I knew that most of their chirps were too high for Gemma's ear.

When I caught the signature whistle of a large male diving deeper than the rest, I called to him, beckoning him to come down. I didn't invite the whole pod, figuring that a hundred dolphins descending upon us might startle Gemma. A wise choice, considering that she jerked as if electrocuted when just one ten-foot-long, thousand-pound bottlenose plunged toward us. He turned aside at the very last second to show us his pale belly as he whizzed past. By the time he circled back, Gemma had seen enough of him to realize what he was. This time, when he brushed by, she stood rigidly, arms clamped to her sides as if to give him room to pass, and yet her expression was the most incredible mix of emotions I'd ever seen — petrified, elated, and awestruck all at once. Maybe I should have called down the whole pod.

The dolphin left us just as we reached a steep embankment. Gemma didn't seem to mind the limited visibility so much now since she bounded her way to the top of the hill without waiting for me. Once there, she stopped short.

I swam up beside her and saw why. The landscape below was filled with giant bones carelessly flung about by scavengers that had devoured a whale carcass — weeks ago, by the look of it. Cartilage floated through the water in ghostly wisps. I gave Gemma's fingers a squeeze and led the way to the edge of the embankment. Gripping her hand even tighter, I leapt off the rocky pinnacle.

We floated down the side of an enormous rock face, narrowly avoiding the massive sandstone peaks that jutted up from below. When our dive boots touched the seafloor, the silt erupted with life. Hagfish squirmed out of the muck and over our boots like a thousand snakes. The ooze under our feet was the last of the decomposing whale flesh, only now it was putrefied, so that only the hagfish could suck it up. Gemma kicked her way upward, away from them. That's when her lack of swimming skills became obvious. Instead of continuing to kick her feet or use her hands to stay afloat, she stopped moving and sank toward the seafloor again. I couldn't help but grin at her efforts. And once she'd caught my silent laughter, she resigned herself to walking.

As we passed under the giant skeleton, I started clicking again. Sensing something square and hard-walled off to our left, I decided to make a quick detour before heading for the Peaveys'.

Still holding Gemma's hand, I led her toward the ugly two-story building. I could see Seablite Prison with my eyes now, dark and abandoned. The first time I'd piloted over it years ago, I'd thought it was a Topside relic from the early twenty-first century because of all its angles and corners. One that had somehow survived the subsea landslide that swept most of the flooded buildings into Coldsleep Canyon. Now, facing Seablite head-on, I saw that it was an odd hybrid of Topside and subsea architecture. Hovering over the seafloor, balanced on tall pylons, clearly it had been constructed down here. Its small windows were round and made of acrylic glass, just like those on old submarines. An air lock shaft dropped from the bottom floor to the seabed.

Above the rusted-open door glowed the "unsound structure" symbol. On the Topside, nearly all the buildings along the coast displayed a yellow circle with a black lightning bolt shooting down its middle, though that didn't stop fierce tribes of squatters from living inside the half-submerged skyscrapers.

As we neared, Gemma pointed at the yellow circle. I shrugged and continued forward. The 'wealth had lied about it being a science lab. I was pretty sure the "structurally unsound" part was a lie, too. The building looked stable enough. When Gemma pointed again, I realized that she was looking above the neon symbol at letters etched into the metal wall, which read: SEABLITE.

My parents would forbid me to go poking around inside; I knew that. But maybe I'd find some information or a clue to help the settlers catch the outlaws. Making up my mind, I motioned to Gemma to wait by the lift lock. Before I got two steps, I was yanked back by the belt. When I turned I could barely see her face, only the shake of her head. I'd forgotten—there was no way she was going to just sit back and wait.

The elevator inside the lift lock wasn't working. However, there was an open hatch in the elevator's ceiling. Swimming upward, I slipped through it. Gemma tried to follow. She gave a valiant effort, but despite all her kicking, she couldn't get herself off the ground for more than a moment. I considered leaving her at the bottom of the lift lock for her own good. What if I was wrong about the building's stability? Still, she'd chosen to come. . . . On her next hop, I caught her by the hand and hoisted her into the elevator shaft.

Luckily, she wouldn't have to swim up the shaft; a ladder was mounted to the inside wall. We climbed to the first level, where a set of elevator doors stood open. The entire floor was flooded. I sent clicks upward and saw in my mind that the water ended halfway up another set of open elevator doors. I motioned to Gemma that we should continue up the ladder.

As I pulled myself up to balance on the last rung, I broke the water's surface and stepped out of the shaft. The sea had flooded the second story of the building but only up to my waist. Gemma emerged right behind me. As my helmet light illuminated the darkness, I rapped my knuckles against the nearest wall. There was no bounce, no give to the old-fashioned solid metal, which seemed sound enough.

The screen on my wrist flashed NORMAL for oxygen level, so I unsealed my dive helmet. Gemma did the same and I freed my flashlight from my belt. I swept the light over the rivets and iron girders as dribbling water echoed through the chamber.

"Can I hold the flashlight?" Gemma asked through chattering teeth.

I passed it to her and together we took in the strange scene around us. The walls were dark and wet. The ocean leaked in, drip by drip, through seams in the ceiling. In the waist-deep water, old diveskins and Liquigen packs floated past as if they'd been dropped just yesterday. Gemma directed the flashlight at the door across the room with bars on its window and then illuminated a wall where several pairs of corroded handcuffs hung from pegs.

I sloshed over for a closer look. "Why are these so long?" The chain between the cuffs was at least two feet in length.

"So the inmates can work," she replied. "There's a penitentiary in the tower block that faces mine. Every day, guards hustle men into the outside elevators and take them down to the dark alleyways." She touched one of the long chains. "The convicts wear handcuffs like these, so they can clean up garbage."

"These prisoners weren't cleaning up anything." I plucked a floating sieve out of the water and ran my fingers across its wide-spaced holes. "They were panning for black pearls."

"That doesn't sound so bad."

"Would you want to hunker in the ooze all day, straining mud?"

"Well, if you put it that way . . ."

"It's backbreaking work."

"I'll bet the outlaws got sick of it and that's why they escaped," she said, sounding excited by the idea.

"Or they got sick of the noise." The creaking and scratching had bothered me since we'd entered. Every shift of the surrounding water and underlying muck made the metal hull twist and compress. Maybe the architecture was part of the prisoners' punishment. Who wanted to live in squared-off rooms with hard walls? It was unnatural.

I splashed into the next room—the guards' station. I checked in the half-submerged file cabinets.

"What are you doing?" Gemma asked. The beam of the flashlight did strange things to the stainless steel furniture in the room, made it gleam and glimmer.

"Looking around." All the drawers were empty.

"Oh, no, you're not." She hopped onto a submerged metal desk. With her legs crossed, she looked like she was attending a tea party, except that she was up to her waist in seawater. She eyed me expectantly.

"What?"

"Your Dark Gift!"

I wondered if it was too late to say I lied just to get her to jump out of the sub. One glance at her face told me not to bother.

"Why do you keep it a secret?" she asked. I sloshed toward the open door at the back of the room, but she was faster. She jumped down and barricaded the doorway with her outstretched arms. "So what if people find out that you can do this cool thing?"

"All the pioneers will leave the ocean and no new families will ever come subsea, that's why." I ducked under her arm and waded into a dark corridor. "My parents work hard for what we have," I said over my shoulder, "same as everyone down here. You think I want to be the reason the settlement fails?"

She fell into step beside me. "At least tell me how it happened. Did you just wake up one morning and realize you could talk to dolphins?"

"I can't talk to them." I caught her impatient look. "Okay. Dolphins and whales can hear my clicks. And when I hear theirs, I can tell what kind of call it is—happy, danger, food. But we're not having a conversation."

The corridor was lined with closed doors—a cellblock. I tried the first one on the right but it was locked. Gemma aimed the flashlight into my face like an interrogator.

"All right," I relented, lifting a hand to shade my eyes. "It didn't happen overnight. After I turned nine, the ocean got noisier and noisier. But nobody else thought so. I noticed more sounds out of water, too, so I just figured my hearing was getting better. After a while, I could tell the difference between an original sound and its echo, so I began to make noises and judge distances that way.

Then, one day, it all came together and I realized that I could see what I heard."

"Why? What were you doing?"

"Nothing. Lying in bed with my eyes closed," I said, remembering every detail about that morning, "and Ma called me to breakfast. When I answered her, I heard my voice bounce around my room. And then I realized I could see my room, without opening my eyes."

"Glacial!"

"No. It was weird."

"Did you tell your parents right away?"

I hesitated. Did I want to dip into the rest of it? Not even a toe. "Yes," I admitted finally. "I told them." I focused on trying another door, but it was locked, too. When I turned back, she was standing in my path again.

"And?" she asked.

"And they hauled me Topside and took me to a slew of doctors." My throat was so tight, soon I wouldn't be able to swallow. "After weeks of blood tests and brain scans, the doctors couldn't find anything wrong, but they wanted to keep poking at me." That was putting it mildly. "The hospital wouldn't release me and then child services got involved. My parents had to go to court to get me back, and even then it looked like the judge might rule against them and make me a ward of the 'wealth. So I pretended I couldn't do it anymore."

"The doctors believed you?"

"I doubt it. But they couldn't prove anything. When I use my sonar, they see activity in a part of my brain that most people don't use. When I don't use my gift, there's no activity. They couldn't justify keeping me any longer. I'm just lucky my real name wasn't in the files. That doctor who wrote that article you're always on about—Doctor Metzger—he never even met me. He heard about the court case and then got all his information from the hospital files. My parents were furious about it."

"But they know the truth, right? That you can still do it."

Turning away, I tried another door. The knob turned but the door stuck.

"You lied to your parents?"

I threw my weight against the door and it fell off of its corroded hinges, slamming to the floor. I barely kept my balance as water gushed past me, flooding into the room. Instead of shining the flashlight into the darkness ahead, Gemma continued to shine its beam on me. "I get it. You don't want to be some medical experiment but—"

"There's no but," I snapped. "The doctors blamed the water pressure, said it was messing up my brain. They told my parents to move to the Topside permanently. Well, I got a good look at how you people live—like hagfish, piled on top of one another. No offense, but I'd rather risk brain damage."

"They're your parents!"

"Not mentioning something isn't the same as lying."

"What are you? Six? Of course it is." She sloshed into the room.

"Good to know where you draw the line," I scoffed. "Lying is bad but stealing, that's just a neat trick your brother taught you."

Turning her back on me, she explored the room with the flashlight. Clearly the conversation was over. Too bad it hadn't ended sooner.

I followed her past the bunk beds that lined the room. Most of the mattresses were missing but blankets and sheets dangled from the bars, like laundry strung up in the darkness. The flashlight's beam slid across the posters taped to the walls. A graphic of a parasailer. Comic book illustrations. A photo of a little girl with strawberry blond hair and a gap-toothed grin.

The weight of the ocean compressed the hard-shelled building, causing it to creak and groan. "Let's get out of here. I'm not going to find out anything about the outlaws in here. Nothing that makes sense anyway."

With her back to me, Gemma returned the flashlight's beam to the photo taped to the wall by an upper bunk. She sloshed closer for a better look. "Probably some prisoner's daughter," I guessed, coming up behind her. Shoving the flashlight into my hands, she clambered onto the top bunk. Carefully, she picked at the tape that held the photo in place. Her movements were jerky, feverish. What was she doing? Her breath came out in short bursts as she peeled the last corner of the photo from the wall.

"That's you!" I said, suddenly understanding. She cradled the picture in her hands. "Why didn't you tell me your brother was in prison?"

"Don't you get it?" Her voice cracked. "This wasn't a prison."

Shining the flashlight at the posters once again, I saw what she meant. Parasailers and comic illustrations. Those weren't images that grown men taped by their beds. Especially not hardened criminals. "It was a reformatory," I gasped. This was where Eel got his shine. Pretty, too. They were the ones who'd worn the handcuffs and panned for manganese nodules.

The walls emitted a metal-on-metal screech that stiffened my spine, and suddenly I remembered that Doc once had firsthand contact with the inmates of Seablite. He'd monitored their health. Last night, when he told the story of the outlaws' escape, he'd known that they were underage boys at the time. Younger than me. Yet Doc had led us to believe they were grown men, had called Seablite a prison—even though no one put thirteen-year-olds in prison. Or did they?

"I don't get it." I struggled to find the reason behind Doc's misrepresentation. "Why would the 'wealth force kids to live down here?"

Gemma's expression turned bitter. "Space is precious." Drawing up her legs, she huddled on the top bunk with her long braid wrapped around her neck like a collar. "The 'wealth isn't going to waste an inch of it on juvenile delinquents."

"Your brother spent four years in here?" Glancing around the dismal room, I felt a trickle of sympathy for the boys who'd formed the Seablite Gang. No wonder they kept robbing supply ships. If I'd been locked up in here, I'd be mad at the government, too.

Gemma pressed her forehead into her knees as if to block out my question. Or maybe she was trying hard to deny the obvious conclusion: that Richard might be in the Seablite Gang. Shivering, she clasped her arms around her legs. Her diveskin was on the fritz because it was too loose on her. Unless it wasn't the frigid air making her tremble.

I waded closer. "Are you okay?"

She shook her head.

Maybe a Topsider would know what to say to her. But I just stood there, stymied and feeling useless, wondering if I should touch her arm or if she'd take it the wrong way.

"Please," she whispered without raising her face, "just leave me alone."

CHAPTER

NINETEEN

With an ache behind my eyes, I swam along the dark corridor on Seablite's first level, which was completely flooded. Gemma probably thought I didn't care that she was miserable, which made me feel worse than if she knew the truth—that I was just plain stupid.

I touched down and a cloud of sludge rose off the floor. A door stood open. I didn't want to bother Gemma just yet, so I figured I might as well look around. I squeezed past the door but before I even got a glimpse of the room, the ugly snout of a grenadier slammed against my helmet. I batted the fish aside and glided forward. My crown lights bounced off metal cabinets and an examination table, giving the underwater room an eerie glow. Circling in place, I realized I was in the infirmary.

I staggered back and my skin grew clammy. I'd entered unprepared—hadn't steeled myself. Now feelings of panic and loneliness entwined within me, the way they always did when something triggered memories of my time in the hospital. But just as my anxiety was smothering the here and now, a low vibration rolled through the room. It was gone before I'd gotten the chance to listen carefully. I hovered, hoping I hadn't imagined it. And then it came again. My ears caught the sound as it intensified, and I relaxed. Somewhere outside, not too far away, a humpback whale was singing. Closing my eyes, I let the music reverberate through me. Hopefully, one floor up, Gemma was listening and the whale song comforted her as much as it did me.

When the lone humpback began a new chorus, I calculated that the animal was about a mile away and coming closer. An idea came to me. A crazy, wonderful idea. I swam through the open elevator doors and up the shaft, surfacing at the top of the ladder as the whale's song died away.

That's when I heard Gemma scream for help.

I dove under the water and swam into the guards' station. Silently, I broke the surface to see her hunkered on top of the desk. The same instant, she caught sight of me rising from under the water and splashed backward, dropping her flashlight and unsheathing her jade knife.

"Gemma, it's me!" I scrambled to unfasten my helmet. "What's wrong?"

"Why didn't you walk through the door like a normal person?" she demanded, once she'd caught her breath.

"I swim faster than I walk. Are you okay?"

Just then, the whale began singing again. She grabbed

my arm. "Do you hear it?" Careening around, she looked for the source of the noise.

Now I understood why she'd panicked. "Let me guess. You think that's a ghost."

Slow realization spread over her face. "It's a whale, isn't it? A stupid whale."

"Whales aren't stupid." My sense of humor was returning.

She raised an eyebrow and pointed toward the corridor where a glowing light darted under the water. "I suppose you know what—"

"Lantern fish."

Maybe I shouldn't have cut her off like such a know-it-all because she frowned as if I'd planted the lantern fish there just to frighten her.

"You told me to go away," I reminded her.

"I didn't know there was going to be inhuman howling along with a glowy thing chasing me. Anyone would have thought it was a ghost."

"Chasing you?"

With her hands on her hips, she was clearly not amused. "You knew I'd be scared out of my wits within five seconds, didn't you?"

"No, I di—"

She steamrolled over my words. "Then you came back so you could split your diveskin, laughing at the dumb Topsider."

"If that were true, I would have brought friends." I scooped up the flashlight and handed it to her. Just then the whale's singing grew louder. "Come on! He's almost here."

I took her by the hand and pulled her toward the elevator shaft—glad that she didn't yank her fingers out of mine. "Whales are curious." I flipped my helmet into place. "If we go outside and turn on our crown lights, maybe he'll come over for a look."

"Why on earth would we want that?"

I snapped her helmet shut and fastened it for her. "Just let yourself sink," I said. Together we breathed in Liquigen and jumped into the dark water that filled the shaft.

Once we were outside, the whale's song was even louder. Gemma clamped her hands over her dive helmet as if covering her ears, while I unspooled the rip cord in my belt. It had clips on both ends and was coated with soft rubber. I fastened one end of the rip cord to my belt, then looped the other end and clipped it to the main line. I could see the whale was still a ways off, plowing along about forty feet above the seafloor.

When our crown lights didn't slow him down a whit, I mimicked a humpback's short, social clicks. Sure enough, the enormous creature stopped singing through his two blowholes and angled downward. With his long side fins flapping, he came straight at us, all thirty-plus tons of him. He wasn't too pretty head-on, with his face covered in whiskered bumps and scars that were probably carved by an orca's teeth. I checked Gemma's reaction. She seemed stunned but didn't back away.

Just before the whale reached us, he sent out what felt like a sigh of greeting. The sound was lower than even I could hear, but I sensed the water's vibrations. Maybe Gemma felt the low-frequency wave as well, for she seemed to relax as it rolled over her and even smiled when the whale passed just above our heads. Struggling to stay upright in his slipstream, Gemma reached up and, touching the fifty-foot humpback without fear, trailed her fingers along one of the grooves that ran from his chin to his barnacle-covered belly.

I got into position so that just as his tail pumped downward, I slipped the makeshift lasso over his flukes and wound the rip cord around my forearm. As soon as I pulled the lasso tight, the slack in the cord spun out. Grinning, Gemma threw her arms around my neck and pressed close. An instant later, the line jerked taut.

For a timeless second, our eyes met and I could see that Gemma's excitement matched my own, and then we were swept off our feet. We flew through the water, laughing and whipping back and forth in the whale's wake, with me holding on to the rip cord and Gemma holding on to me.

CHAPTER

TWENTY

Just outside the Peaveys' bubble fence, I released the lasso from the whale's tail and Gemma and I touched down on the seafloor. Pushing past the bubbles, I led her through the kelp field, only to stop before we reached the last row. At her questioning look, I pointed at a hovering sub that had just arrived, trailing a loosely drawn net filled with rockfish. As a throng of settlers gathered to unfasten the net and unload bins, we slipped into the hustle unnoticed.

I pointed out my mother and Gemma watched as Ma pried the lid off a container. A cloud of blue burst out of the box—a school of full-grown shad. Every family in the territory had brought some of their own livestock to replace what Shurl and Lars had lost. Spotting us, Ma smiled and waved. I knew she thought that we'd just come from the Trade Station, having retrieved Gemma's duffel bag. Now I was going to stir up her fears again by telling the other settlers about my run-in with Shade. Around us, my neighbors signed to one another, rapid-fire. I wondered if Gemma realized that they were asking about her.

Lars darted about shaking hands while settlers swam up to the moon pool and climbed into the house. Trying to follow the crowd, Gemma hopped but sank immediately back to the seafloor. Rather than remind her to release the fins in her boots, I signed upward at the settlers by the moon pool. Instantly, a rope ladder unfurled, nearly hitting her on its way down. I tugged it straight and offered her the ladder with a grand sweep of my arm. I thought my teasing might annoy her, but she surprised me with a grateful smile before clambering upward to the house.

Inside the wet room, settlers unhinged their helmets and towel dried their diveskins until the metallic fabric gleamed. I nodded and answered everyone who called out my name or smiled at me, but my gaze was on Pa across the room, speaking to a cluster of settlers who hadn't been at yesterday's meeting with Representative Tupper.

Perched on the lip of the moon pool, Gemma took a deep breath to clear her lungs while looking about curiously. I hoped she wouldn't say anything about the other kids' shines.

Gasps of surprise and dismay exploded across the room, followed by angry exclamations of "They can't!"

and “What does that mean for us?” Clearly Pa had just broken the news about the Commonwealth’s decision to abandon the territory. Heart constricting, I set my boots and helmet against the wall.

“Ty,” Gemma whispered, “those little kids are staring at us.”

“At you.” I set her helmet next to mine.

“Why?”

“Jibby told you yesterday and you didn’t believe him.”

Across the room, Pa headed upstairs with a contingent of angry settlers. Those who were left set about cleaning up the equipment bay.

“Hey, Pete,” I called to a neighbor. “Is Doc here?”

“Yeah. Upstairs.” With a smile, Pete added, “Howdy, Gemma.”

Her mouth dropped open. But in a flash, she recovered and returned his smile. “Okay. I get it,” she said to me. “Down here I’m a rarity.”

“Some might even call you an oddity.”

Her eyes glinted with pleasure as if I’d just paid her a compliment.

“Behind you,” I said as the surface of the moon pool began to churn. Gemma whirled to see a black shape rising out of the water and scrambled to her feet. “It’s a sub,” I assured her, “not another scary singing whale.”

She gave me a shove.

The sub's hatch opened and Mamie called out, "Who's going to give me a hand with all this food?" Instantly, a line formed and the platters and bowls were passed from one person to the next, out of the hatch and right up the stairs.

"Did she make all this herself?" Gemma asked as she handed me a sea pineapple pie.

"No, all the families contributed something. Mamie went around and collected it all to bring today. It's easier to unload one sub," I explained.

"Gemma!" Jibby nudged his way into line between us. "How do you like Benthic Territory?" He passed a platter of crab cakes to me without peeling his gaze from her.

"I love it!"

"What part?" I was shocked. In one day, she'd witnessed a knife fight, escaped capture by outlaws, and discovered that her brother had been sent to a subsea reformatory. Not exactly Benthic Territory at its best.

"This." With a wave, she indicated the line of talking settlers.

"Want to stay subsea permanently?" Jibby asked. "I've got a hundred acres."

When Gemma's brow crinkled with confusion, I gave her the translation. "He's asking you to marry him."

A laugh caught in her throat and came out as a cough. "I'm too young!"

"Oh. Well . . ." Jibby's face fell. "It just gets awful quiet with no one else around," he mumbled.

"You're always welcome at our place," I said. "You know that."

He ignored me. "Hey, I know. How about you come visit for a while. As long as you like," he told Gemma. "I've got three empty bedrooms. You can have your pick. Heck, take the whole house. I'll move into an outer-building."

When she didn't reply immediately, I broke out of line to face her. "You're not considering it?"

"A whole house?" she asked pointedly. "I've never even had my own room."

I couldn't tell whether she was teasing or not. Spinning on my heel, I headed for the stairs. "While you plan your visit, I'm going to ask Doc about that place we found."

"Not without me!" Thrusting a seafood casserole into Jibby's hands, she ran after me.

"That's a standing invite," Jibby called out. "Good anytime."

The main floor of the Peaveys' house was packed with settlers, clearing away the last of the mess. In the living room, Doc stood with a group of settlers in grim discussion. I couldn't bring myself to question him in front of others. I was too angry about being lied to. So I was relieved when Shurl waylaid me and thrust a plate into my hands. "Ty, will you start the buffet line? The food is getting cold. And Gemma, honey, take two helpings of everything. A tide pool could drag you under."

I followed orders since the more I thought about it, the more I realized that discussing Seablite in front of Gemma might not be a good idea now that she knew that her brother was one of the "escaped convicts" in Doc's story.

After serving ourselves from the bounty laid out on the dining room table, Gemma and I joined Hewitt and Zoe on the stairs that led up to the bedrooms. Beyond the windows, the boundary lamps dimmed until they resembled pale moonlight.

"Why do you look so glum?" Gemma asked, taking a seat next to Hewitt. "I can't believe how quickly your house got put right."

"Lucky me." He picked at the crab claw on his plate.

"You didn't really think your parents were going to move Topside, did you?" I asked, settling two steps up. "They're tougher than that."

"But I want to live where I don't have to do chores all day, along with schoolwork. Topsiders"—he pointed at Gemma—"don't have to do anything. They push a button and they have food. Flick a switch and the garbage is gone. Turn a knob and friends come over."

"Really?" Zoe nudged Hewitt to sit next to her. Instantly, he scooted up a step.

"Don't ask me," Gemma said, shrugging. "I'm not your average Topsider."

"It's that kind of lazy living that made a mess of this planet," I snapped. "People wanted everything to be easy and disposable. Look where it got us."

"Why aren't you like other Topsiders?" Zoe asked.

"I'm a ward of the Commonwealth."

"So?" Hewitt turned his back to me.

"Well, it's just that families pay for their kids to live in boarding homes," she explained, "while I get moved into whatever dorm has an empty bed that month." She went on quickly, "It's okay. Most of the time, I'm in with the little girls and they're fun." She grinned. "I taught the six-year-olds every bad word I know."

I got as far as, "Please don't—"

When Zoe yelled, "Teach me!"

"— teach them to Zoe," I finished.

She threw her arms around Gemma. "Ma and Pa will adopt you! They always wanted more kids, right, Ty? They did," she continued as if I'd answered. "But they didn't have any more because Ma got too scared after Ty went to the hospital."

Hewitt became absorbed in pushing peas across his plate.

"Thanks," Gemma said, smiling. "But I'm going to live with my brother."

"You still have to find him. What if he's not even in Benthic Territory?" Zoe asked.

Shooting me a pained look, Gemma said, "I know he *was* here. I'm just not sure what he's up to now."

"Stow it, shrimp." I wanted to get Zoe off the topic of Gemma's brother, but also, I wanted to hear what the raised voices in the other room were saying.

Raj Dirani's snarl rang out loud and clear. "Representative Tupper said dead or alive. Next time someone sees the *Specter*, I say we torpedo her."

"I'll be right back." I set my plate aside. Quietly, I slunk down the hall and into a corner of the kitchen in case my parents thought that I wasn't old enough for such talk. The adults had paused in their task of restocking the cabinets to form a casual circle.

"You'd kill them without a trial?" Ma asked hotly. "Even if Representative Tupper condones it, it's vigilante justice, which isn't justice at all."

Scowling, Lars touched the bandage on his head. "We have the right to protect ourselves."

"If we start ignoring the law," Pa said, "this won't be a community worth saving. I'll join a posse—so long as our intent is to find the outlaws and turn them over to the Maritime Rangers."

"Think a judge will convict them?" Doc asked evenly. At Pa's scowl, he put up his scarred palms. "All I'm saying is you know the legal system is overloaded. The mainland prisons are packed to the rafters. Same with the penal ships. Unless the evidence is rock solid, the criminal goes free."

"Doc's right," Lars said. "We know what we know. But we don't have proof. We can't even ID them. Their dive gloves don't leave fingerprints and they keep their helmets darkened when they're robbing supply ships."

"Not Shade." Raj pried his seaweed cigar from his mouth. "Pretty hard to miss an albino in a lineup."

"Shade isn't albino." The words tumbled out of my mouth before I'd thought it through. Everyone in the kitchen turned to look at me.

"Why do you say that, son?" Lars asked.

My gut plummeted. I had planned to tell the others about my discovery, but this wasn't the time or place. There was a ferocity in Raj's expression that scared me.

"John, your boy says Shade ain't an albino," Raj growled. "What's he know that we don't?"

"I already told Ranger Grimes what I know," I stammered.

Raj mashed out his cigar in a cup. "That dryback has chum for brains. He couldn't hook a fish swimming in a bathtub."

"Tell us exactly what you told him, Ty," Lars demanded.

Taking Gemma's words about keeping secrets to heart, I spilled all of it. How I came face-to-face with Shade in the kelp field and then recognized him in the Saloon. I didn't even leave out my encounter with him in the elevator or the sub chase, although I saw my parents exchange a look that froze me to the core. I knew what they were thinking—that I couldn't be trusted to follow their rules and keep myself safe.

"Why would Shade use zinc-paste?" Shurl asked when I finished my story. "Why not just darken his helmet like the rest of the gang?"

"Because you'd know him by his size if you ran into him," Lars growled. "You'd suspect anyway. But if you think the man's an albino, you focus on that."

Raj unholstered his pistol. "Big don't stop a harpin," he said, checking that its barrel was loaded with mini harpoons.

"This discussion has gone far enough." Ma sent a stern glance around the group. "Raj, put the gun away."

"Sure," he said, holstering it. "But it's coming out again as soon as I hit the Rec Deck." He turned to Lars. "You coming?"

"A mud slide couldn't stop me. Let's round up some of the others, too."

"Shade isn't there now," I pointed out. "I told you, the *Specter* came after us." My words had no effect on them.

They stormed out of the kitchen, leaving me torn up inside, not sure whether I'd done the right thing by telling them. Pa's look of disappointment told me what he thought.

"I'll fetch Zoe and Gemma," Ma said. "We're going home." She and Shurl left the kitchen. Pa, too.

I started to follow but Doc drew me back with a hand on my arm. "Stay a minute," he requested in a low voice. He seemed puzzled by something. Disturbed even. "Describe the man you saw in the Saloon again. The one you think was Shade. Only this time, tell me about his features, not his skin color."

"Why?"

"Indulge me."

That was just about the last thing I was in the mood to do. "I found Seablite," I said instead.

He looked at me sharply but something in my expression must have told him that I wouldn't be put off. "It's not hidden," he said, sounding resigned, and picked up his plate of food.

"It wasn't a prison." I couldn't keep the anger out of my voice. "It was a reformatory."

"Technically," he acknowledged with a shrug. "If you'd met those boys, you'd understand. All of them, sociopaths and criminals."

"They were just kids," I argued. "Younger than me. And the 'wealth kept them on the seafloor in handcuffs."

"Your point?"

"You're lying when you call it a prison. You're covering up what the government did."

Doc's plate clattered onto the counter. "You think I don't want to talk about what happened in there? Think I didn't try?" His dark eyes blazed. "Five years ago, the 'wealth filed the Seablite incident under 'Confidential' and if someone dared mention it, he was stripped of everything he cared about. Me, I got demoted and discredited. So don't lecture me about honesty, Ty. We all have our secrets."

I hesitated but could think of no reason to hold back. "Gemma's brother was sent to Seablite."

Doc turned whiter than a clam. "What was his name?"

"Richard Straid."

Suddenly pensive, Doc rubbed one of his scarred palms.

"You remember him. Is he in the Seablite Gang?" I asked, voicing the worry that had plagued me ever since Gemma found her picture on the reformatory wall.

"No." Doc drew out the word, still deep in thought. "He was the prospector they killed."

Sorrow spread through me like puffer fish toxin. Sorrow for the freckled boy in the photo, but most of all for Gemma.

"The computer made the match an hour ago," Doc

went on softly, now meeting my eyes. "Richard Straid's DNA was in the system because he spent time in a government institution—a reformatory."

"He must have broken out with the others," I guessed, trying to put the pieces together in a way that made sense. "But then Richard went his own way as a prospector. And then what? The gang decided they couldn't trust him?"

"He would have known their real names," Doc agreed.

"So they hunted him down and killed him." I felt sick at the thought of it. Maybe it would be better not to tell Gemma. What was the harm in letting her believe that her brother was still out there, even if she couldn't find him?

"As we just discussed, it's best to be honest when you can," Doc said as if he'd read my mind. "Bring her here and I'll tell her."

"It's okay," said a quiet voice behind us. "I heard."

CHAPTER

TWENTY-ONE

Gemma sat like a sea lily for the ride back to the homestead—still, pale, and fragile. Ma and Pa exchanged concerned looks and whispers the whole way, having been filled in on Doc's news—except the part about Gemma being a runaway. Doc kept his promise and didn't tell, which didn't matter because the viewphone was ringing the moment we climbed out of the moon pool. Pa answered and the face of a woman filled the screen.

"Oh, no!" Gemma ducked behind me. "It's Ms. Spinner. The one who's always moving me around."

Surprised, I looked back at the viewphone. I'd assumed that the director of Gemma's boarding home was a New Puritan. Boy, was I wrong. Ms. Spinner epitomized a very different sort of Topsider by removing everything natural about her appearance. Her overcurled hair shimmered with as many colors as a parrot fish while her features looked as if they'd been drawn on with pastel chalk. As always, the effect creeped me out.

"Are you John Townson?" she asked in an oh-so-nice voice that I wasn't buying.

"I am." Pa sounded like he wasn't buying it, either.

"I'm Eudora Spinner, the director of the Elmira Boarding Home," she said, then tacked on a smile. "I received a call tonight from a Ranger Grimes. He tells me that you may have one of our wards staying with you."

Pa beckoned for Gemma. I wanted to grab her by the hand and hide her away, but I knew my parents would never agree to keep her presence a secret.

As if her body was filled with rocks, Gemma slowly made her way to stand in front of the screen. "Hello, Ms. Spinner."

The woman tsked softly. "Gemma, how could you worry me like this?"

Gemma's attitude remained courteous but she didn't reply.

"Well, it's a lucky thing that the teachers remembered all your questions about Benthic Territory." Ms. Spinner's smile turned pitying. "I suppose you haven't found your brother?"

Stone-faced, Gemma studied her cuticles.

"Have you considered that maybe, just maybe he doesn't want to be found?" Ms. Spinner steepled her fingers as if in thought. "Richard turned twenty-one six months ago. Isn't that right? Gemma, darling, I think it's time you accepted the hard truth: If he wanted to be your legal guardian, he would have come for you already." She sighed dramatically. "I don't know how you manage to keep up your delusions year after year, believing that your brother cares, when he hasn't even bothered to visit you since you were twelve."

"I've caused you a lot of trouble, haven't I, Ms. Spinner?" Gemma asked, sounding remorseful, though I saw that behind her back, her hands were balled into fists. "I do hope you didn't drop any lower on the housing waiting list on account of me. I know how badly you want to get out of your cramped little apartment."

With a wheeze of outrage, Ms. Spinner cracked her polite facade.

"Oh, no, they pushed you down the waiting list?" Gemma exclaimed with mock horror. "I'm ever so sorry."

"Sorry?" Ms. Spinner hissed, with her multihued curls trembling. "I've dropped a place for every hour you've been missing. Believe me, girl, 'sorry' will take on a whole new dimension when you get back."

Ma, who had been standing next to Gemma throughout the call, put a protective arm across her shoulders.

"Ms. Spinner," Pa said, taking up position on Gemma's other side. "We'd like to offer Gemma an alternative. She is welcome to live here with us."

"If she wants to stay subsea," Ma added.

"Out of the question," snapped Ms. Spinner before Gemma had a chance to respond. "We'd never place a ward in an experimental settlement on the seafloor."

Anger propelled me forward. "Sending her to a reformatory is better?"

"Than living with Dark Life?" Ms. Spinner scoffed. "Please. There's no telling what the water pressure is doing to you people. And I'm not going to have that ungrateful girl serve me with a lawsuit ten years from now because she has brain damage. I'm afraid, Mr. and Mrs. Townson, you do not meet the Commonwealth's qualifications for suitable foster parents."

A muscle ticked in Pa's jaw and I knew it was taking all of his restraint to keep his temper in check. "We may not be living subsea much longer," he said.

I felt my bone marrow harden.

"Well, when you've established yourselves back in civilization, feel free to fill out a foster care application. In the meantime, Miss Straid," Ms. Spinner said, fixing her sharp eyes on Gemma, "you will be at the territory's Trade Station tomorrow by seven A.M. Ranger Grimes has kindly offered to escort you to your new living assignment."

"Which is?" Gemma asked in a hollow tone.

Ms. Spinner smiled unpleasantly. "The Altoona Reformatory for Wayward Girls. I have no doubt you'll feel right at home with the other charges."

Gemma didn't wait for the viewphone to cut to black; she fled up the stairs.

CHAPTER

TWENTY-TWO

I couldn't move. Straps bit into my arms and legs, holding me down. I lifted my head and saw that I was belted to a hospital bed, shirtless and shoeless. I thrashed, making the straps cut into my flesh, but still they held me in place. From out of nowhere a gas mask appeared, hovering over my face. I twisted away, my neck cramping with effort. Steely fingers gripped my scalp as the mask covered my nose and lips. I choked back my cries, holding my breath. Rolling my eyes upward, I saw a man in a surgical cap, pressing down on the mask. Foul gas pierced my lungs. My vision blurred and . . .

I jerked awake in the dark, drenched in a cold sheet of sweat. Another nightmare. When would I be done with them? Turning on my side, I listened to the house—to the soft hum of the generator and air purifiers. That helped slow my heart. I got out of bed and pressed my forehead to the cold window. Nothing suspicious lurked in the kelp field. Suddenly a splash one level down broke the silence. A familiar enough noise, but not one that I often heard in the middle of the night. Who would be climbing in or out of the moon pool at this hour?

I hurried down the stairs, noting that the wet room lights were off. Worry dug into me. I swung around the center pole of the staircase and landed with a soft slap of bare feet on the lower level. The only light illuminating the wet room was from the boundary lamps surrounding the property and they were set on dim. Still, I could see Gemma across the room, digging through the contents of a locker—probably looking for her diveskin since she was wearing Zoe's too-short nightgown again. The minisub bobbed in the center of the moon pool, which relieved me. Using the clamp to pluck up a minisub, swing it over the moon pool, and drop it directly into the water was tricky enough in a bright room. But as far as I could tell, she hadn't scraped up its side or cracked its viewport on the hard edge.

"What are you doing?" I asked as I flicked on the lights at the bottom of the stairs.

She whirled, looking guilty and bedraggled.

"You're running away again," I said. Seeing her duffel bag by the moon pool hollowed out my chest.

"I was just borrowing your sub," she stammered. "I couldn't think of any other way to get to the Trade Station. I was going to leave it there."

"What would that get you?"

"I'll hitch a ride to the mainland on some wingship or houseboat. Or stow away."

"Don't stop at the Trade Station," I said, wishing I could control the catch in my voice. "You could run into Grimes. Go all the way to Paramus and then leave the sub at the Seaguard pier. We'll pick it up there."

"You're going to let me take your sub?" she asked, confused.

"How can I stop you? I'm not going to shoot you."

"You could wake up your parents."

"Right. Zoe, too. Then all four of us can sit on you until the Maritime Rangers show up."

She relaxed. "That doesn't sound fun for any of us."

I nudged her duffel bag with my foot. "Did you take food?"

When she shook her head, I scooped up a sea grass basket inside the greenhouse door and tossed it to her. Then I plucked two apples from the nearest tree and flipped those to her as well. "I'm really sorry about your brother."

She nodded but didn't meet my gaze. As she dropped the apples into the basket, she murmured, "You're a lot like him—the way you look out for people. Richard did that. Not just for me but for the boys in his dorm. He'd stand up for them even if it meant getting himself into trouble." She looked up with sudden inspiration. "Come with me."

"To the mainland?"

"No, farther. You don't want to be stuck living Topside. Let's buy a boat with the money Richard sent me and sail away."

"Where?"

"Anywhere. How about the Colorado Islands?"

My ears grew hot at the thought of us together on a boat. "I can't."

Her eyes drifted to the window behind me. "Ty . . ."

I braced myself. I didn't know how else to say "no" when the idea was so appealing.

"You said the outside lights never turn off all the way." She pointed over my shoulder. All around the homestead, the boundary lamps flicked off, one by one. I bolted for the window. The last lamp cut out and the fields went dark. Gemma pressed in next to me. "What's happening?"

The kelp close to the house was still illuminated by the light from inside. Except for one dark patch, I noticed, which was the house's shadow. No, that wasn't possible. The house was the light source, so it wouldn't cast a shadow. Something else was out there, one story up. The shadow grew darker and wider. Whatever it was, it was descending.

I pressed my face to the window, trying to see upward, but nothing dropped into view. Too bad I couldn't use sonar through the thick flexiglass. Whatever was one story up now maintained its position. I backed away from the window. Whales didn't hover and sharks didn't come in that size of big.

"Ty?" Gemma followed my gaze. Then, as she leaned in for a closer look, something enormous and dark plunged past the window. She jerked back with a gasp.

My heart kicked into high gear as I grabbed hold of her hand.

"What was—" she asked as I dragged her through the fruit trees.

"Outlaws." I yanked open the greenhouse door and we ran for the stairs only to skid to a stop in the center of the wet room as the shadow glided by another window—this time close enough to blot out all else. Faster and faster, the *Specter* circled. Like a shark closing in on its prey. Pulled by the swirling water, the house twisted on its anchor chains, making us stagger to keep our balance.

"Go!" I shouted, steering her toward the stairs while I raced for the house speaker and punched the button. "Pa, wake up!"

"Ty? What's going on?" My father's voice was alert. No doubt he'd been shaken awake when the house started moving.

In the background Ma cried, "John, the boundary lamps are out!"

"The *Specter* is circling us," I told them. "I think the outlaws just shut off the exterior power, but I don't know how."

Pa's response was a curse that would have made a miner blush. "Where are y—" His voice cut out, along with every noise in the house. And every light.

"Ty!" Gemma was only halfway up the stairs.

"It's okay." The backup generator would kick on in an instant. Even though it hadn't at the Peaveys', it would be different here. This was my home and I knew how every inch of it operated. But seconds passed and all I heard were my parents' frantic footsteps on the floor above. Finally a strip of red emergency lights flickered on around the moon pool while outside tiny green lights outlined the struts of the house. My tension eased as I waited for the air purifier's familiar hum to start up. Then I remembered all the emergency lights ran off a battery pack. The backup generator remained as silent as a corpse.

Dread sloshed in my gut. It was the same nightmare all over again. Like Shurl and Lars, we were going to lose our livestock, our crops, and our house within thirty minutes. I tore off my T-shirt, tossing it into the changing room as I ran past.

"What are you doing?" Gemma leaned over the railing, her face pale in the scant light.

I paused below her. "Everything will be okay. The outlaws will steal a few things like they did at Hewitt's. Then they'll leave." At least I hoped so anyway. But part of me wondered if I'd brought this upon us. Shade had threatened to kill me if I told anyone else about him, and I had. What if he was here for me?

"Ty!" Pa shouted from above.

"Down here!" I called back. "Go wake Zoe," I told Gemma. "Then lock yourselves in her bedroom. Don't open the door until you hear me on the other side." Without waiting for her reply, I ran to the far side of the room, threw open my gear locker, and grabbed my diveskin.

My parents pounded down the stairs, both sealing their diveskins as they squeezed by Gemma, who was finally headed up.

"The *Specter* is coming around the starboard side," I told them as I shucked off my sweatpants and stepped into my diveskin.

The *Specter* shot by the window on the far side of the wet room, leaving a storm of bubbles in her wake. "They're trying to scare us so we'll stay inside," Pa growled. "They'll probably go for the equipment and supplies in the outerbuildings."

"What do you want to do?" asked Ma as she holstered her speargun.

"I'll tell you what we're not going to do, and that's give over anything without a fight," Pa vowed.

Ma gave a crisp nod as she pulled two Liquigen packs from the slots in the wall and tossed one to Pa.

When the *Specter* cruised by the closest window, I shrank back. She was circling so tight, it seemed like she would shear the acrylic skin right off the house. Somewhere inside that sub was Shade, a realization that sent an icy finger skimming down my spine.

Ma handed me a shockprod. "Join the girls upstairs."

"No way. I'm as good a shot as both of you. And I've got sharper water eyes for sure."

"Yes. But I mean to have you see sixteen!" Ma said in a low, fierce voice.

"We need him, Carolyn," Pa cut in. "Guard the moon pool," he told me. "Shoot anything or anyone who tries to surface."

"Except you."

Pa flashed a wry smile. "Except us."

Ma caught my arm. "If too many are coming in, don't play the hero. Especially if one of them is Shade. There's no shame in hiding. You hear me?"

"If it's Shade, I'm taking the shot."

My mother didn't argue. She followed Pa into the moon pool, speargun in hand. As they slipped under the water, a panicky chill spread through me. Soon sharks would come to feast on the dying livestock. My parents would be facing predators in the dark—both fish and human. But I wasn't helping anybody standing here, stiff with fear. I rushed up the stairs to check that the girls were locked into Zoe's bedroom, only to find them hovering at the top of the stairs in white nightgowns and anxious expressions.

"This is my fault," Gemma whispered. "This wouldn't be happening if I hadn't dragged you into the Saloon."

"You went in the Saloon?" Zoe asked in a voice so loud I flinched.

"You didn't drag Hewitt into the Saloon and they attacked his homestead," I pointed out. If it turned out to be anyone's fault, most likely it would be mine. "Go." I waved them back toward the bedrooms. "Lock yourselves in."

"No." Gemma held up her jade knife. "I want to help you."

"Keeping Zoe safe helps me."

Zoe gasped with indignation. "I can take care of myself!"

Gemma met my eyes over Zoe's head and nodded in answer to my silent plea. "Ty just said that so I wouldn't feel bad," she told Zoe. "Really, he wants you to look out for me. I'm the dumb Topsider." She put an arm around Zoe and gently tried to steer her back down the hall.

Zoe was having none of it and ducked under her arm. "I'm coming with you," she told me. "I want to see an outlaw." Darned if she didn't sound excited.

"You'll put Ma and Pa in danger," I whispered angrily. "If an outlaw snatches you up, they'd die trying to save you." Zoe actually looked frightened at that. I took full advantage of it. "Go to your room, bolt the door, and barricade it." As the girls backed down the hall, I heard a splash in the wet room.

I crept down the stairs, shockprod up. It was dark in the wet room despite the emergency light strips in the floor. Still, I could see that an oval shadow floated in the moon pool. I sent out several clicks, hoping I was wrong. But no, my sonar confirmed what I'd already guessed. Next to the reaper bobbed the Slicky—hatch open. Instantly I knew how Shade had found me. It was sickeningly easy. He'd simply climbed into the Slicky and hit the HOME icon. Fear whispered through me. Shade was in the house. The *Specter*'s circling—that was just a diversion to get my parents outside. Now, somewhere in the dark, Shade was waiting to strike.

Thuds ran along the window to my left. I whirled to see a school of tuna thrashing against the glass. A hammerhead shark plowed through them and carried one off. Where were Ma and Pa?

I couldn't think about it right now. Shade was close. That fact kicked everything else to the edge of my brain. I crept toward the equipment bay, clicking as I went. All I could make out were vehicles. Of course, sonar couldn't tell me if something was hiding behind them. Taking another step, I put my bare foot into a puddle of cold water. The shocking chill of it shot through my body and sharpened all of my senses. My parents had made no splash when they slipped into the water. The puddle came from someone climbing out of the moon pool, dripping as he went.

I should be scared, knowing that Shade had come to kill me, but it was anger that surged through me, hot and sharp.

Why hadn't I changed weapons before checking on the girls? To use the prod, I had to touch the tip to my target, and I had no intention of getting within arm's reach of Shade. I cast out more clicks and sensed nothing but equipment. In the dim green light, the metal foam walls cast an eerie glow.

Summoning up my grit, I hurried toward the weapons rack, only to trip over something in my haste. Lifting the soft clump with the tip of the shockprod, I tried to make out what it was.

A sharkskin vest.

If I'd held a single doubt about Shade's presence, this doused it. I shook off the vest like it was the shed skin of a reptile, holstered the prod, and ran for the weapons rack. There my fingers skipped over the standard-sized speargun and instead curled around the cold steel of the biggest harpoon gun Pa owned. With two hands, I hefted it from the rack. It was a man-sized gun, heavy and long. Pa kept it for the rare occasion a shark burst through our bubble net. I didn't like the idea of shooting a human with it, but I had no choice. A small harpin might not stop Shade unless it hit him dead through the heart.

Edging into the center of the room, I sent my clicks out again. I listened for their echoes and saw the wet room in my mind as clear as if every light in the house was on high. And there was the intruder, emerging from behind a sub, pressed close to the wall. He was invisible to my eye. But in my mind, the shadow across the room was a three-dimensional outline of a man. A man so big and tall it could only be Shade. My sonar was so sharp, I could even tell from the echoes bouncing off him that his chest was bare: The outlaw's flesh had a sharper echo than the fabric of his pants.

Shade flicked on a small flashlight, aiming it at the floor and then the walls to get a quick read on the room. My heartbeat slowed as I realized I had the advantage. Shade couldn't see in the dark. So long as I stayed out of the flashlight's beam and away from the emergency lights, he wouldn't spot me.

I lifted the end of the harpoon gun, bracing the butt against my shoulder. The muscles in my arms trembled as I struggled to hold the heavy gun steady. I threw out another series of clicks, then took aim with my mind's eye. It was going to be hard because Shade was moving quickly along the wall. But if I didn't hurry, in another minute, he'd be at the stairs. It would be much harder to find him, let alone get a clear shot, on the second floor with its many rooms. I inhaled, clicked once more, found my target, and pulled the trigger.

The gun's kick sent me flying backward as the harpoon launched. The instant I landed on the floor, there was a crack of steel puncturing acrylic accompanied by a strangled cry. The harpoon had hit its mark. Had I killed him? The thought made me shudder.

Scrambling up, I saw Shade's flashlight roll across the floor. Clicking, I gagged over the picture formed in my mind: Shade thrown back against the wall. Pinned there. The harpoon jutted from his left arm, just below the shoulder. His breath came out in pants as his struggling stilled. My sonar couldn't tell me why Shade had stopped moving. Was he passed out? Or just faking it to lure me closer? Whirling, I ran for the other side of the wet room, slipping in the puddle of seawater along the way. I needed to know how much of a threat Shade was at this point. Snatching an emergency lantern from its hook, I unholstered my shockprod.

I set the lantern on the rim of the moon pool, where it would illuminate the whole room. Facing the wall where Shade was pinned, I flipped on the lantern. The sight that met my eyes froze me into place. Every inch of his flesh was red. So were his eyes. Blood? I tried to make sense of the terrifying vision in front of me. Too shocked to register that Shade had wrapped his hands around the harpoon until, with a pained yell, he yanked its pointed tip out of the wall behind him. Pressing his palms to the butt of the harpoon, he pushed its length through his arm, screaming as he did.

The sound of the harpoon hitting the floor jolted me back to reality—Shade was free. And coming for me.

I lifted the shockprod. But I'd missed my chance. Shade raced toward me, turning from red to black until he was nearly invisible again. I should have cut the light to give myself the advantage, but he was nearly on top of me before I had a chance.

I spun, aiming the prod at the outlaw circling me, but with the moon pool at my back, I had nowhere to go. Closing in, Shade wrenched the shockprod from my grip, throwing it across the room where it clattered against the gear lockers. I went for my knife, but Shade was too quick. He ripped my knife from my belt and flung it into the moon pool. Before I could slip into the moon pool as well, he threw me down so hard that white-hot pain flashed through my brain as my head thumped onto the floor.

I forced myself to stay conscious. The glow from the lantern played over Shade's skin, black and slick. As I scuttled backward through the puddle, his eyes reddened until his pupils were slits of fire. Stomping on my chest, he pinned me to the floor with his bare foot. "Where's the girl?" he snarled.

I shook my head. He'd have to kill me before I gave up Gemma and Zoe. A drop of Shade's blood spattered onto my cheek. As I whipped my face aside to escape his dripping wound, a movement caught my eye. Through Shade's legs I saw Zoe peering through the spindles of the staircase.

Gemma grabbed Zoe by the arm and tried to pull her back up the stairs. Zoe twisted and tugged but Gemma hauled her up, step by step, almost out of sight until . . . Zoe bit her wrist. Hard. When Gemma's hand sprang open and she fell back, Zoe tore downstairs. Shade turned at the noise. Clawing at his leg, I tried to free myself, only to have him grind his foot down harder.

Zoe stopped on the bottom step, in her nightgown, with her curls wild and a toy shark clutched in her arms while Gemma slipped out of sight at the top of the stairs.

"Get off him!" Zoe's voice was shaky but ripe with warning.

Shade's gaze dragged over her. "Sweet," he drawled. "But not the one I want. Where's the other girl?" When I didn't answer, he bore down with his foot so hard, I choked with pain. "The one from the docking-ring."

"Stop it!" Zoe yelled.

"Tell me," he warned. His pupils widened until his eyes were entirely red. "Or I'll ask the angel over there."

"Go ahead and ask me, jerk face."

"Zoe!" I croaked while waving her away, only to cry out as one of my ribs cracked under Shade's heel.

"Where"—the outlaw spat each word—"is she?"

"Here!" Gemma stumbled down the stairs and stepped in front of Zoe, blocking her from the outlaw's view. "Please don't hurt them." She threw down her jade knife.

With a curl of his fingers, Shade coaxed her forward. When I squirmed with renewed effort, he glanced down as if deciding whether or not to kill an insect. Shade was going to take Gemma and there was nothing I could do to stop it. . . . But someone else could.

"Zoe!" I gasped. "Do it!" Between Shade's legs, I saw her scoot around Gemma. "Now! Touch the—" My words ended in a scream as Shade's foot bore down and cracked another of my ribs. Despite my agony, I forced my eyes open to see Zoe kneel next to the puddle that had spread across the wet room floor. She dipped her finger into the water.

A second later, a tsunami of pain hit me as electricity blasted through me, frying every nerve ending in my body. Above me, Shade spasmed as if caught in a lightning storm, and then stiffened. When he collapsed, a second wave of pain crashed over me and my world went black.

CHAPTER

TWENTY-THREE

I woke with a burnt taste in my mouth and an awful toothache. Someone was sobbing nearby. It had to be Zoe. I didn't have to see her to know that she was rocking on the balls of her feet with her head thrown back and her mouth wide open. No one else in the world could howl like that. One of her pets must have died. I opened my eyes to tell her I'd help her catch a new monster if she'd just quit making that awful noise.

I blinked against the harsh light and abruptly Zoe's howls stopped. Closing my eyes, I decided to use my sonar instead but as I turned to send out clicks, my side burned with pain. Groaning, I squinted at Zoe, who gaped back at me in astonishment. Then she slid out of sight as my bed rolled forward.

Not a bed—a gurney, I realized as the fog lifted from my mind.

"You'll need to leave the room now," a voice said. Doc's voice.

Something was binding my chest so tightly, every breath was a shot of pain. Still, I tipped my head back, only to see that I was being pushed into a metal cylinder.

"You're awake," Doc said. "Lie still. This won't hurt at all."

As the cylinder drew closer, strange lights flickered inside of it. Panic seized me as memories shrieked like ghosts in my head. I was headed into an MRI scanning machine. Thrashing onto my side, I set my broken ribs on fire.

"Ty, don't move," Doc commanded.

Lifting my head, I saw him, tight-lipped with determination. I tumbled off the gurney, gripping the edge in case my legs wouldn't hold me—but they did. Wearing nothing but a hospital gown, I ran for the door. "Come back!" he shouted after me.

Pushing through the swinging door, I burst into the infirmary to find my family gathered by a row of beds. Gemma, too. When my parents saw me, they rushed forward. Pa got to me first and eased me onto a bed before I collapsed.

Doc shoved through the door, eyes on me. "Are you crazy?" Turning to Ma and Pa, he said, "He ran out like I was killing him."

"Give him a minute, Doc," Pa said, giving my neck a reassuring squeeze.

Ma sat down on the bed next to me. Her fingers trembled as she gathered one of my hands into hers and rubbed my knuckles down her cheek. Across the room, Gemma nervously rolled the infirmary's crash cart back and forth like she was rocking a cradle.

"Who knows how much electricity surged through him?" Doc said. "I need to check his brain for damage and—"

"No!" I said.

A movement at the end of the bed caught my attention. It was Zoe, clutching her toy shark as if her life depended on it, still in her nightgown. "Please don't die," she whispered.

"I'm not going to die," I scoffed.

"I didn't mean to hurt you." A sob broke her words, making them hard to understand.

In a blinding flash, the events of the night burst into my mind. My fear, the searing pain as my ribs cracked . . . and Shade. Most of all Shade. Towering and terrifying with his glowing-ember eyes. "Shade," I gasped, throwing my legs over the side of the bed. Ma's hand tightened around mine, holding me back.

"He's locked up," Pa assured. "Ranger Grimes will take him to the coast within the hour and we'll never see him again."

My gaze flew to Gemma, who looked as wracked as I felt. What had she told everyone?

"What's this?" Ma asked, sounding alarmed as she touched my arm.

Glancing down, I saw an odd feathery mark that started on the inside of my elbow and bloomed upward over my bicep. It looked as if someone had traced my capillaries in purple ink.

"A Lichtenberg bruise," Doc said. "Ranger Grimes says Shade has one just like it."

Running a finger over the intricate pattern, I winced as pain erupted along my skin.

"People get it after being struck by lightning," Doc explained. "But any kind of electrical shock can cause it." His gaze settled on Zoe.

She squirmed and opened her mouth to speak, but I got the words out first. "That was really smart of you, shrimp," I croaked. "Putting the shockprod in the puddle. Really smart."

Across the room, Gemma stopped rolling the cart and frowned.

"Yes," Zoe whispered, backhanding her tears away. "I did that."

"You said you didn't remember what you did," Doc corrected.

"She was scared," I cut in while keeping my eyes pinned to my sister. "She picked up the prod from the floor. Probably didn't even realize what she was doing." Zoe nodded, lips pressed into a tight seam. "I told her to put it in the puddle," I added.

Doc crossed to stand in front of Gemma. "Did you see what happened?"

"Is there a problem, Doc?" Pa asked.

"I'm gone for good in forty-eight hours." Doc's gaze bored into me. "If there's something wrong with you, now is your chance to find out. After that, you're on your own."

I stiffened with anger. "There's nothing wrong with me." As if I'd trust him anyway after he'd purposely misled us into thinking Seablite was a prison.

"Let's give Ty a little time and then see how he's doing," Pa suggested.

"He's a kid!" Doc turned to Pa. "He doesn't know what's for the best. Don't you have some control over him?"

"Some," Pa said wryly.

"Not to have him examined is negligence. Pure negligence." With that, Doc stalked out of the room.

"Now that Shade has been arrested," Ma said quickly, covering the awkward silence, "everyone thinks the rest of the gang will clear out of here. I thought you'd want to know, we're reconsidering our move Topside." She smiled and handed me a pile of folded clothes. "Maybe the 'wealth will even offer a reward for his capture."

I looked at Pa, who smiled back. It was enough to make my ribs stop hurting for a moment.

Once they left the room, I hurriedly stepped into a pair of drawstring pants. As I tore off the paper gown, the feathery bruise caught my eye. I sank to the bed as I faced the fact that this bruise was the second thing that Shade and I had in common. There was no denying it anymore, not after what I'd seen. Shade had a Dark Gift.

Cheers and applause broke out when I swung open the door to the dining hall. Jibby, Raj, and the Peaveys raised their tankards. "To Ty!"

Jibby thrust a cup into my hand. "We're celebrating Shade's capture."

"What time is it?"

"Middle of the night," Shurl replied, beaming at me.

Sidling close, Gemma whispered, "We need to talk." She led me to an empty table.

Good, now we could get our stories straight.

"You have to tell them Dark Gifts are real," she said once we settled on top of the table.

"What? No!"

"People need to know that Shade can camouflage himself."

"Why? He can't break out of jail by changing the color of his skin."

"You're setting an example for Zoe and Hewitt," she scolded. "Probably other kids, too. They watch you because you're older. And what are you telling them? To be ashamed of themselves."

I glanced at Zoe, who seemed younger than usual, curled in Ma's lap, clutching her toy shark. I looked away and ignored the guilt seeping into me. "I'm sick of people watching me. The settlers watch to see if I'm healthy, because if I am, they think they don't have to worry about their kids. Topsiders watch to see if the water pressure is affecting me. I don't want to be a prototype—I want to be normal."

"But you're not," Gemma said. "You're different. Special. You may as well admit it. And just so you know, it's not normal to want to be normal. People who are normal want to be special."

"Yeah? Down here, *you're* special. So special, an outlaw wanted to steal you away. But just so you know, the opposite of normal isn't special. It's abnormal. And I'm not admitting that to anyone. Ever. All it would get me is a one-way ticket Topside and more medical exams. No, thanks."

"I need you, boy," said a voice from behind us. I turned to see Ranger Grimes standing nearby. He smirked at Gemma. "You think you fooled me yesterday? I ain't been out here so long I don't know a female when I see one. Young or not."

I stepped between them. "I thought you were taking Shade to the coast."

“That’s right. But first”—he clapped my back—“I want you to ID him as the lowlife who almost killed you.”

“I was there, too.” Gemma hopped off the table. “And conscious the whole time. Isn’t my ID worth something?”

“Sure,” the ranger said with a shrug. “Come have a good long look.”

CHAPTER

TWENTY-FOUR

"Where are we going?" Gemma asked when the elevator stopped at the Access Deck.

The elevator doors opened facing the huge window of the exterior corridor. The ranger's skin took on a greasy sheen as he stepped into the passage. "I put him in the storage bay."

"Shade's dead?" I asked with a start.

"No," the ranger scoffed. "If the shock didn't kill a stringy bit of jerky like you, you think it's going to kill that hunk of meat?"

"Why put him in storage?" I asked as Gemma and I trailed behind Grimes.

"Had to keep him somewhere," the ranger muttered, glancing uneasily at the sea outside the window. "The 'wealth gives Doc all the fancy medical equipment he wants. But do I get a jail?" He took a bottle of pills from his coat pocket and downed two without water.

"Are you okay?" Gemma asked.

With shaking hands, Grimes pulled out another bottle of pills. Capsules this time. He broke one apart and poured the powder onto his tongue, wincing at the taste.

I stopped short. "You're seasick!"

"So?" The ranger wiped the beads of sweat from his brow. "That's how a normal person feels when he's forced into an underwater death trap." Hustling around the corner, he headed for the storage bay.

I followed him. "That's why you wouldn't check out the Saloon yesterday. Because you're scared to come down to the lower station."

"Sick don't mean scared," the ranger snapped.

Maybe not always, but going by his expression, sick sure meant scared in his case.

He slipped a key into the large padlock on the double doors. Pushing open the door, he waved us inside. I dropped my arm in front of Gemma, blocking her way. "Is Shade walking around loose in there?"

The tips of the ranger's ears reddened. "You think I'm an idiot, boy?"

I met Gemma's eyes and we both pressed our lips tight to keep from smiling. "No, sir." We stepped into the cavernous room. Maybe the ranger wasn't an idiot, but he didn't know about Shade's Dark Gift—hadn't seen him blend into the background so thoroughly he was nearly invisible.

"Keep moving," the ranger directed as the doors swung closed behind us. "He's way in back."

Lightbulbs dangled from the ceiling in widespread intervals, casting barely enough light to see the fronts of the cages that lined the walls. "Settlers rent the stalls for storing extra stuff," I explained to Gemma as we headed down the center aisle.

"Not just settlers." The ranger directed us around the end of the aisle. In the far corner was a freestanding cage, half in shadow. "I'm sure the marine biologist who's storing it won't mind us putting it to good use," he chortled. "The bars are made of pure titanium."

A shark cage.

Gemma hung back in the shadows. "I don't want him to see me."

I nodded. Shade would probably haunt her dreams as it was. I followed the ranger into the pool of light.

"Show yourself so this boy can ID you," the ranger called into the cage.

No reply.

The ranger banged a white stick against the bars. "Step forward or I'll taze you twice as long as last time."

There was a sound of someone getting to his feet. A crate flew across the cage, into the light, and crashed into the bars. With a yelp, the ranger jumped back.

"Just moving my seat," a deep voice said. Then Shade stepped into the dim light. His skin was once again coffee brown and badly pockmarked. Black tattoos wound up his neck and over his skull. He wore only pants, having left his vest on our wet room floor. He probably preferred being bare chested—the easier to camouflage himself. Just as long as he didn't do it in front of Grimes.

Blood seeped through the bandage wrapped around Shade's left arm. If his wound hurt, he sure didn't let on. Dropping a heavy foot onto the crate, he rested his right arm across his knee, revealing the feathery bruise etched on his forearm. "How are the ribs?" he asked in a mockingly pleasant tone.

"Yes." I faced the ranger. "He's the one who broke into our house."

"You sure you saw me, kid?" Shade asked.

"Yeah, he's sure," the ranger snapped. But then Grimes stumbled backward, teeth bared in a grimace. "What the—"

I reeled to see Shade's eyes frost over until they were solid white. He threw himself against the bars, sending me skittering back. "Are you sure you saw *me*?" he demanded as his skin burst into a million pinpoints of light.

The ranger shouted out. Or was that Gemma, who was still hunkered in the shadows?

I peeled my gaze from Shade's dazzling light display to see Ranger Grimes scrambling for the aisle. As he rounded the corner, his uniform caught on the edge of a storage cage. Frenzied, he ripped his sleeve free of the wire and disappeared. His running footsteps echoed through the storage bay until there was a distant swoosh of the door opening. When it slammed shut, I felt my carefully constructed reality crack like a seafloor rift.

Now everyone would know that Dark Gifts were no myth. Irrefutably. My jaw clenched as tight as my fists and I whirled on Shade. "Did you have to show it off?"

With his skin still radiant, he leaned casually against the bars of his cage. "Why do you hide it?"

I glared at him without answering.

"What do you care what people think?" he asked.

"You're going to care when the ranger comes back, bringing the others."

"That worries you," Shade observed. "Know why?" he asked softly.

I braced myself for another one of his tricks. Sure enough, his face smoothed out and his pockmarks disappeared. Then every inch of his skin began to shimmer until it was reflective, like liquid mercury. Even his eyes. He'd turned himself into a human mirror. Now my own reflection stared back at me—scared and intense—superimposed onto Shade's skull. *That's crap*, I wanted to yell, but my throat closed off. I was nothing like him. Nothing. The man was a violent outlaw. He'd killed Gemma's brother.

"Flaunt it, kid." Shade's skin darkened and his tattoos reappeared. "Make 'em get used to it."

"You're giving me advice?"

"You make a good poster boy." His tattoos spread like spilled ink until every inch of him turned black—even the whites of his eyes. "That helps all of us. Including you."

"I don't need help. I'm not the one in a cage."

"Not all cages have bars. A reputation can cage you." He was nothing but a rumbling voice now. "So can a secret."

"So can being an outlaw."

His snort of amusement rang in the darkness. "We tried to make it Topside. But the boys lack social skills. Had to get them away from civilized people." The outlaw's smile floated inside the cage like the Cheshire Cat's. A grin without a face. "Mostly we hit government ships. I figure that while we were in Seablite, we dug up a million dollars' worth of black pearls. Never saw a penny of it and got nothing in return. Not even schooling. The 'wealth owes us."

"You nearly destroyed the Peaveys' farm." I paced in front of the bars. "Did their homestead look like a government ship?"

"I said 'mostly.'"

Rustling told me that he was moving away as if finished with the interview.

"You're good at making excuses," Gemma said from her hiding place in the shadows. "Got one for killing my brother?"

The instant she spoke, Shade's skin rippled with light. She'd startled him. I felt a tinge of satisfaction. The outlaw wasn't superhuman; he hadn't sensed her presence.

When she stepped forward, her rage electrified the air. "His name was Richard Straid."

Color washed over Shade like a breaking wave, leaving him brown-skinned and tattooed again. He reached into his pants pocket. "Him?" Shade held up a photo—Richard's. "Found it in the minisub we hauled in yesterday."

With a cry, Gemma shot forward. "Give me that!" She jammed her arm between the bars.

"Gemma, no!"

A smile floated over Shade's mouth as if he was pleased by her spunk. But within a blink, his expression iced and he grabbed her by the throat. "Get the key," he bellowed at me. "Now!"

When I didn't move, he tightened his grip on Gemma's neck and forced her to face me. The despair in her eyes tore at my heart.

"If you're not back in five minutes," Shade warned in a voice as deep and cold as the abyss, "she'll no longer be breathing."

CHAPTER

TWENTY-FIVE

"Like hell I'm going back in there," the ranger spat, sweating and shaking as he loaded his sub into the moon pool. "If that girl is too stupid to stay back, she deserves what she gets."

"He's going to kill her if you don't open the cage!"

"You tell me what that was." The ranger rounded on me.

"What?" I asked, confused.

Grimes grabbed a fistful of my shirt and gave me a shake. "Doc was right, wasn't he? Living down here does something to you people."

"Doc never said that!"

"No? I got a report in my office by Dr. Metzger that says otherwise. That was Doc's name before he changed it to Kunze."

I gaped at him. Doc wrote that article? Was that what he meant about trying to tell the truth of what happened in Seablite?

Smugness took Grimes's anger down a notch. "Didn't know that, did you?"

"Doesn't matter," I said, steeling my expression. "Whatever name he goes by now, Metzger was proved a fraud."

"No, boy. The government called him a fraud so people would keep on immigrating subsea. But I know better." Grimes pulled me close. "Now you tell me what that outlaw can do."

I struggled to free myself from the ranger's grip. "He can change color. That's all I know."

"But it could be more. More than changing color . . ."

I thought about Zoe and her power to stun a shark with electricity or fry a man. I nodded.

The ranger released me so fast I stumbled backward. "You got one, too, don't you?" he spat. "A Dark Gift."

"No. I—"

"Shut up." His glare was packed with hatred and fear. "I'm not going back in there." He yanked a tazer from his holster. "Hit him with this and he'll let her go real quick."

"Shade is using her as a shield and the cage is backed into a corner. There's no way to get him without hurting Gemma."

"You're the freak. You figure it out." Grimes jumped onto the bumper of his sub and threw open the hatch.

Furious, I grabbed hold of the sub's hitching line. "Give me the key."

"So you can let him loose? Not for all the space in the 'wealth. I'll send a ship of rangers back to get him."

"Think this post is bad?" I yanked the hitching line and sent Grimes lurching to keep his balance. "If Shade kills a girl while in your custody, imagine where they'll send you next."

With the key gripped in my fist, I raced through the storage bay. When I rounded the corner at the end of the aisle, I saw Shade had moved Gemma next to the door of the cage. The outlaw smiled at me while she kept her eyes down.

"Where's the ranger?" he asked as I neared the cage.

"Grimes wants nothing to do with you." I held up the key.

He smirked as if I were a small child elaborating on a big lie. "He's outside, waiting for me to step through the door, gun in hand," Shade guessed. "Question is, did he have time to call in more guns?"

"I brought the key, now let her go." I drew back my hand to throw him the key.

Shade slammed a shoulder into the bars. "Don't. You come here."

I inched closer. "It'll be okay," I whispered to Gemma, even though Shade stood right behind her. As soon as I got the cage door unlocked, he shoved it open. Before I could jump back, he grabbed my arm and threw me to the far side of the cage, all the while keeping a grip on Gemma. Stepping out, he took hold of her with his other hand and kicked the door shut. The heavy lock snapped into place.

"Don't leave him in there!" Gemma cried.

Ignoring her plea, the outlaw led her around the corner and out of sight. I heard him say, "Call to the ranger and tell him you're coming out alone. Then push open the door." He said more but his words were too muffled to make out.

The storage bay door creaked open. I pressed against the bars. "Grimes, he's out there! You just can't see him!" But the only response I got was the swoosh of the storage bay door swinging shut in the distance. I kicked at the lock on the cage. The scene played in my mind: Shade, camouflaged against the metal foam walls, slipping down the corridor to steal a sub and escape.

The silence stretched out forever. Would he take Gemma as a hostage? I shuddered at the thought. Suddenly the storage room door banged open and running feet slapped the hard floor.

"Ty!" Gemma sprinted around the corner with the key in her hand. "I'm coming!"

CHAPTER

TWENTY-SIX

"Shade knocked him out with his own gun," Gemma explained as she slipped her hand under the ranger's jacket.

"Don't bother checking for a heartbeat. He's breathing," I said, getting to my feet. "Just make sure his head isn't bleeding. Be right back." I ran down the corridor and into the enormous wet room, where there was a viewphone. I called Doc and gave him a quick rundown of what had happened.

"I'll sound the alarm and tell the others that Shade is loose," he said. "Stay with Grimes. I'll be right there."

By the time I ran back down the passage, Grimes had not only woken up but was struggling to stand. "Let go of me," he snarled at Gemma, who was trying to hold him down.

"You're hurt," she said.

"Doc is on the way down," I told him. "He should take a look at your head. That was a bad blow."

Pushing Gemma's hands aside, he heaved himself to his feet. "My head is fine. And so's my memory," he said, casting me a meaningful look. "So don't try to tell me—"

A Klaxon horn cut him off as it screeched through the entire Trade Station, announcing a Red Alert. Even if Grimes claimed his memory was fine, he looked confused now.

"That's for Shade," I explained. "He escaped. . . ."

The ranger wheeled around and headed for the wet room.

"Where are you going? Doc's on his way."

"And he ain't going to find me here," Grimes said over his shoulder.

Gemma's eyes met mine. "Well, it's not much of a bump."

Still, I followed Grimes to the edge of the moon pool, glancing around the wet room as I went. What if Shade was hiding somewhere in here? Being the middle of the night, the Access Deck was deserted. Anyway, most people moored their subs along the inner docking-ring of the Surface Deck. I could imagine the chaos up there right now, set off by the Red Alert. Not that there were many people aboard the Trade Station at this hour, only those drinking in the Saloon or bunking in the Hive. The Klaxon horn had surely interrupted their R & R.

"You're leaving us with an outlaw on the loose?" I demanded as Grimes climbed into his sub.

"You're the idiot who let him out," he replied and then ducked into the cockpit and slammed the hatch.

"That doesn't excuse you running away," I shouted, though I knew he probably couldn't hear me. As his sub sank under the water, I looked around the empty wet room and didn't see Gemma. The image of the blood-soaked wet room in her brother's rig floated up in my mind and a chill settled over me. I hoped Gemma had returned to the Service Deck and joined my parents.

When I finally made it to the dining hall, I found Hewitt and our families there. Ma rushed over to me. "Doc said you two were okay, but he didn't have time to give us the whole story. What happened down there?"

"How did Shade escape?" Lars demanded.

I ignored their questions and scanned the empty tables in the dining hall. "Gemma isn't here?" I asked, trying to curb my panic.

"No. Not since she left with you," Ma said.

Behind us, the door swung open and Jibby entered. "I've never seen a place clear out so fast." Raj barged in right behind him.

"Who's left?" Lars asked.

Raj shrugged. "Us."

"Did you see Gemma anywhere?" I asked.

Both shook their heads.

"I'm going to check the Surface Deck," I told my parents.

"We just came from there," Jibby said. "It's deserted."

"You should have seen it." Raj smirked and unholstered his harpistol. "All them boats and subs launching at the same time, over one little escaped outlaw. Cowards."

"How's Ranger Grimes?" Pa asked me.

"He left."

"Left?" Shurl asked. "With a prisoner on the loose?"

"Wouldn't even wait for Doc to bandage his fool head," I replied.

"Looks like we're on our own." Raj sounded oddly happy about that fact as he loaded miniharpoons into his gun.

"I just don't comprehend how an outlaw that size snuck up on Grimes," Lars said. "The ranger may be a bigot but he ain't blind."

When the group looked to me for an answer, my stomach twisted. "I was locked in the storage bay. I didn't see it." Which was true, but Gemma was right: Withholding information was a form of lying. "I need to find Gemma," I said and slipped out of the canteen.

I raced down the corridor, only to turn the corner and see the elevator doors closing. I pounded the call button. Eyes pinned to the screen, I was surprised when the elevator stopped at the Recreation Deck. But Raj had said the Trade Station was empty except for us. . . .

When the elevator finally returned, I saw the name on the adult ID card jammed into the slot and knew exactly who'd gone to the Saloon, even if I didn't know why. The card belonged to one Ranger Matt Grimes. Nice. Gemma had pickpocketed an unconscious man.

The moment I stepped onto the catwalk, I spotted Gemma three stories down, pacing the Saloon floor. The whole place was dark and deserted, though half-full tankards littered the tables and seaweed cigars smoldered in the ashtrays. I ran down the first stairladder and paused at the top of the second. Just as I opened my mouth to call down, a movement behind her tightened my throat. A dark figure peeled away from the window. Shade! Advancing on her, he brightened with each step.

"Behind you," I croaked. But it was too late. Like a striking cobra, Shade's hand shot around her face and covered her mouth. Straddling the stairladder's banister, I slid to the first catwalk. I had no weapon. No way to stop him from hurting her. I hit the grilled floor and sprang to my feet. "Leave her alone!"

Shade turned her to face him. I dashed toward the opposite side of the hanging platform to the stairs that led to the Saloon floor, chancing a look over the rail as I ran.

As Gemma gazed up at Shade, his skin smoothed out and his dark color drained away—including his coiling tattoos—leaving him pale. But not albino. Aside from his bandaged wound, only his feather-shaped bruise marked his skin. My own arm ached along the points of my matching bruise. I skidded to a stop at the top of the last stairladder. Why wasn't she struggling to get away? Shade's grip on her was loose. Gentle. He glanced up. As his eyes found me they blanched to solid white and then the centers blossomed into blue. And all at once, I understood.

Shade was Gemma's brother.

He was a very different Richard than the one in the photograph, but even with his shaved head and bulging muscles, the man standing before her was obviously her brother—pale, freckled, and blue eyed. When his transformation was complete, Gemma threw her arms around him and I felt sick to the core. Had she known he was Richard all along? The way she was hugging him sure meant it wasn't new information.

Unable to tear my gaze from their reunion, I descended, moments replaying in my head, taking on alternate meanings. The dark figure on the docking-ring—that was Shade watching Gemma pull off her disguise. Maybe that's when he recognized her. So when the *Specter* chased us, he wasn't after me; he'd been trying to catch up with Gemma. And last night, when he'd invaded our homestead, he'd come for her.

Nausea gave way to anger, as I realized how I'd been duped to aid in his escape. My feet hit the Saloon floor with a dull thud, echoing the feeling inside my chest.

Gemma whirled and saw me. After a moment of silence, it was clear she didn't know what to say, so I filled in the words for her. "That was a great act you put on tonight. You really had me believing you were scared out of your skin."

"I didn't know he was Richard! Not until you went to get the ranger and we were alone."

"Right," I said, even though there was nothing right about any of it.

"How could I have known?" she asked and then turned to Shade. "Why didn't you tell me who you were last night?"

"I wanted to get you alone. The rest of the world thinks I'm dead." He shot me a hard look. "And it better stay that way."

What did his not-so-subtle threat matter? I now believed Gemma didn't know who he was until half an hour ago, so I felt somewhat better. Not a total sap.

"You spilled your own blood inside that sub?" Gemma asked him. "But Doc said no one could lose that much and live."

"He saved it up," I guessed. "Froze it, pint by pint, over time."

Shade grinned. "Knew you were a smart kid."

"What good does it do you?" I asked angrily. "You're still wanted as Shade."

"The rangers ain't my worry. I got a bigger threat hanging over me. You got the same one, you just don't know it."

"Like I'm going to believe anything you say. The Commonwealth is pulling out of the territory because of you and your gang."

"Best thing that could happen. You don't want to be dependent on the 'wealth, kid." His tone turned sardonic. "Someone might take advantage of the situation."

I glared at him.

"Ty, please," Gemma begged softly. But I couldn't bring myself to think of this outlaw as her brother. Even light-eyed and freckled, the man radiated danger, had Shade's hypnotic voice.

"You get the money I sent?" he asked, giving her braid a tug.

She nodded.

"It's clean. Not stolen. Put it away for school."

"School?" she scoffed. "I'm coming with you."

Surprised, he dropped her braid. "This is a visit, nothing more."

"I didn't come all this way and risk getting eaten for a *visit*. You said we'd have a home of our own someday. With our own quality-time room."

A faint smile pulled at his lips. "You were little when I said that."

"So? Remembering it got me through the weekends when all the families were together," she said. "And the holidays. I didn't mind being alone because you said that when you were grown we'd do all the things that real families do together." She crossed her arms as if to shore up her composure. "On your twenty-first birthday, I waited for you. I had your present and a cake and my bags packed. . . ."

I glanced at Shade but reading his face was like trying to gauge how the stone deities in my room were feeling.

"And when Doc said you were dead and I—" She paused. "Anyway, I was alone again, only this time I didn't have the hope of being with you to make it okay." She met his gaze head-on. "Were you even going to tell me you were still alive?"

"You know I would've," he said and even sounded like he meant it. "But that changes nothing. You're going back to the Topside tonight."

"Why can't I live with you on the *Specter*?"

Shade threw back his head and laughed. It was a deep, rumbling sound like an underwater earthquake. "Live with outlaws?" he snorted. "That's why I gutted fish for three years?"

Gemma stiffened but before she could argue further, a crack echoed through the Saloon and a blinding spotlight caught us in its beam.

"Freeze!" commanded a voice from above as boots clanged on the ladder. Whirling, Shade raced for the window while another spotlight snapped on and followed him. Positioned on the first catwalk, the beam was so bright it was impossible to tell who held it.

"Look at him!" someone shouted as Shade's skin turned translucent green. Though he blended with the window behind him, the spotlight brought out his contours and kept him from disappearing entirely. The second light found him and illuminated his lower half, encased in dark pants.

Storming forward, Shade lifted a bar table and threw it at the man on the stairs who was holding one of the spotlights. With a cry, the man dropped the light and jumped out of the way, landing with a thud. Shade tore toward him, darkening as he went. The beam of the other spotlight chased him across the Saloon as he knocked aside tables and kicked over chairs. The man on the floor screamed as his harpistol flew from his hand, snatched by a nearly invisible fist. Shade paused over the prone man . . . Lars.

A deadly sharp harpoon punctured the top of a metal bar table, sending me and Gemma scooting back.

"Stop shooting," a voice bellowed from the first catwalk. A familiar voice. Although the person was no more than a shadow on the first catwalk, I knew it was Doc.

"Jibby, your wild shots are going to sink us," another voice barked. Raj.

These weren't rangers here to arrest Shade. These were men I knew.

With a running leap, Shade climbed a vertical strut. Hand over hand he went, with Lars's pistol tucked into the waistband of his pants. When he reached the first catwalk, he flipped over the railing. Illuminated by the spotlight, he advanced toward the second stairladder, blanching with each step until his skin glowed ivory white and his eyes burned red. "Move," he growled, putting a foot on the bottom rung.

Still holding the spotlight, Jibby backed off fast.

"You're not going anywhere," Raj yelled down, taking aim with his harpistol.

The spotlight's beam caught Shade on the stairladder, making him the perfect target.

"Stop them." Gemma clutched my arm. "They'll listen to you."

I shrugged off her hand. "He might be your brother, but he's still an outlaw. He deserves to go to jail."

Halfway up the second ladder, Shade lost his footing, crumpling as if he'd been shot in the gut. Doc stepped into the light, holding an air gun used to administer vaccines, but now it was probably loaded with some tranquilizer.

Feet scrabbling for the rungs, Shade clung to the ladder with one hand and reached for the pistol in his waistband with the other, only to twist as if he'd been punched in the shoulder by an invisible fist. His grip loosened, finger by finger, and he fell onto the lower catwalk, making the entire structure swing dangerously.

Gemma sprinted across the Saloon until she was underneath the spot where Shade was lying. Her face was tear streaked and she was breathing hard, but she said nothing as she stared up at him.

"Geez. You were right, Doc," Lars said, amazed. He got to his feet near Gemma. "How did you know she would lead us to Shade?"

Disgust rose like bile in my throat. Doc had known all along that Shade was Richard Straid. And he'd let Gemma think her brother was dead even though he knew we'd seen Shade alive in the Saloon hours earlier.

As Shade rolled to his side, his skin danced with light as if his nervous system had gone haywire.

"He's doing it again," Raj said, banging down the stairs.

Doc closed in on Shade, who struggled to get to his knees.

"How can he do that?" Jibby's voice jumped up an octave.

"I told you," Doc said, aiming the air gun at Shade's chest, "he's not normal."

I cringed.

Sitting back, Shade pulled a thick needle out of his shoulder. "Surprised you're back in the ocean, Doc, seeing as last time didn't go so well," he said. "Destroyed your reputation, right?"

Doc shot another needle into him. Like a silver shard, it glinted between Shade's ribs but he only smirked. "Still sore about your hands? Least I didn't cut 'em off."

I felt sick, knowing that Shade was the one who'd slashed Doc's palms open.

Raj kicked the outlaw onto his stomach. The needle flew from Shade's grip, rolled across the catwalk, and fell through a crack. Gemma jumped aside as it *pinged* on the Saloon floor.

Pushing past me, Lars hustled up the stairs while Raj tied Shade's hands behind his back and took the pistol from him. Both wore the same expression that Grimes had—a twisted look of fear and hatred. Shade's Dark Gift made him a monster, and I couldn't help but wonder if one day they'd look at me that way.

When Lars stepped onto the catwalk, dread shot through me. I looked at Gemma. But with her focus on Shade, she hadn't noticed the rope looped over Lars's shoulder. Or that it ended in a noose.

CHAPTER

TWENTY-SEVEN

"You trying to silence me, Doc?" Shade snarled from where he lay. His words sent Gemma scampering out from under the catwalk to see what was happening up above. "Afraid I'll tell these good folk about how you tested your theories on a bunch of kids?"

"Juvenile delinquents with criminal records," Doc retorted, nodding to Lars, who threw the rope to Raj.

Shade rose to his knees though his hands were tied behind his back. "Orphans. All wards of the 'wealth." His skin rippled, turning bloodred. "Got to experiment on us all you wanted. No one to interfere."

"Shut up!" Doc gestured impatiently and Raj sent one end of the rope sailing into the air where it looped over a steel crossbeam that ran underneath the second catwalk.

I tore up the stairladder, shouting, "You can't do this," even though the ever-present pain in my ribs was a sharp reminder of what Shade was capable of.

When Raj played out more rope, the noose dropped into view.

"No!" Gemma raced up the stairs to the first catwalk.

I hovered by the second stairladder. If Pa were here, he would stop this. But he wasn't, and there was no time to run and fetch him from the dining hall.

"Jibby," Lars yelled. "Get her out of here!"

My heart lurched as Gemma tried to pry Lars's fingers from the railing so that she could get past him. "He's my brother," she argued. They were twenty feet over the Saloon floor, yet she struggled so fiercely that if Lars were to suddenly move aside, she'd fall.

Clamping his spotlight to a strut, Jibby edged closer. "Maybe this isn't a good idea, huh?"

"Are you forgetting about that bloody sub?" Lars asked.

"That was *his* blood." I stepped forward. "He didn't kill anyone!"

Behind Shade, Raj tied the end of the rope to the steel beam that edged the floor of the catwalk.

"We could call the rangers," Jibby suggested in a hollow voice. "Let them take him."

"So he can come back again?" Doc's knuckles whitened as he gripped the rail. "I told you, no jail cell can hold him. No prison."

"You give me too much credit," Shade drawled. "Just because I busted out of your house of horrors. That don't mean much."

"You ain't busting out of this." Raj dropped the noose over Shade's head.

Gemma's anguished cry sparked Jibby to life. He came up behind her and spun her to face him. Before she recovered from her surprise, he muttered, "Sorry 'bout this," and hoisted her over his shoulder like she was the catch of the day. Quickly, he mounted the second stair-ladder with Gemma hollering and pounding on his back.

I positioned myself at the bottom of the stairs in case he dropped her. Upon getting an upside-down view of the Saloon floor fifty feet below, Gemma's fists froze mid-pummel. "Ty, stop them!" She reached back toward Jibby's shoulder. Her hand flashed forward as she dropped something at me. I stepped back and let it clatter to the mesh floor. Her jade knife.

My legs felt like they might fold under me as I picked up her knife. Stop them with a knife? Right. And even if I could, did I really want to? With Shade gone, Benthic Territory would have a chance. Ma and Pa would keep the homestead. All I had to do was . . . nothing.

Above me, Jibby disappeared with her into the elevator and the doors slid shut. Now that the structure was no longer swaying, Raj climbed onto the railing. With one arm around a vertical strut, he caught the noose and drew it in. The thin rail buckled under his weight, cracked where it was soldered to the beam, then snapped. Raj jumped back to the catwalk just in time.

Even though Lars had a harpistol aimed at his temple, Shade shook his head as if to clear it. He was collapsing from the tranquilizer that had been shot into him, but they were going to hang him anyway. Right now. Without judge or jury.

Raj kicked the other end of the railing. After three attempts, the rail broke free and clattered to the floor far below. One jagged piece remained, sticking out from the strut like an ax head.

Horrified, I surged forward but Doc gripped my arm. "We're doing this for the good of the territory, Ty. To keep it going. You want your own homestead, right?"

I did. But not like this.

Raj circled behind Shade and he lifted his boot. The reality of it collapsed on me. He was going to kick Shade off. In the split second that his boot swung back, I jerked out of Doc's hold and sprang between Shade and the edge of the catwalk.

"Ty, move!" Raj bellowed. If he kicked Shade, he'd send me plummeting to the Saloon floor below.

"You don't know what he's capable of," Doc growled.

"No," I agreed. "But I see what you're capable of."

When Shade edged back to give me another inch of room, I saw that under his heavy lids, the outlaw's eyes were bright. The tranquilizer hadn't affected him nearly as much as he was pretending.

Above us, the elevator doors slid open.

It was all the distraction I needed. As the men glanced up through the grill, I raised the jade knife. “Kneel,” I hissed. Instantly Shade fell to his knees, tightening the rope that ran from his neck to the girder. I slashed at it while trying to keep my balance as boots pounded two catwalks up, making the whole structure jump. Still I sawed, acutely aware of the drop behind me. Finally the knife broke through the last strand of rope and Shade sprang to his feet. I spun, only to find myself looking down the barrel of a speargun.

“Step aside, Ty,” Doc commanded. Beside him stood Raj and Lars, their expressions suddenly worried.

“Bring down a judge and I will.” I glanced back to see Shade step through his arms so that his hands were now tied in front of him.

“Son, do what Doc says before you get hurt,” Lars said, sounding anxious.

“If he were like any other outlaw”—Doc took aim at Shade—“we could go by the book. But he isn’t.”

Gemma appeared at the top of the stairladder with Pa and Jibby on either side of her. Others crowded behind them. They wouldn’t make it down the two stairladders in time to stop Doc from shooting. That instant, Gemma gasped and I sensed Shade vanish behind me. I whirled to see that he hadn’t fallen—he’d jumped. Now he dangled from the jagged stub of railing still attached to the vertical strut. Writhing, he used the metal's sharp edge to saw through the rope binding his hands.

"Move!" Doc shoved me aside, aiming the speargun at Shade, who twisted in the air just below us.

I took a deep breath and said loudly, "I have a Dark Gift. Are you going to take away my rights?"

My admission rang through the Saloon. All movement stopped. Ma and Pa froze on the stairs with Zoe and Hewitt clambering down behind them. The posse, men I'd known all my life, stared at me. And so did Doc, except that his look was triumphant. Probably because he'd finally gotten me to admit what he'd suspected all along.

With a loud snap, the rope binding Shade's wrists broke and he dropped to the floor.

Everyone raced down the stairs to the Saloon, except me. I wrapped a leg around the strut and slid down, beating them all. But by the time I hit the floor, Shade was nowhere to be seen.

My parents were the first settlers onto the floor and their expressions were stricken. "I knew it," Ma said. She looked to Pa. "I told you it didn't go away."

"Why did you say you couldn't do it anymore?" Pa asked me.

The other settlers gathered around my parents. Hewitt and Zoe, too.

"You would have given up the homestead," I said.

Ma looked close to tears. "It's just a house."

"The ocean is my *home*."

"Ty," Pa said, "living down here isn't worth it if—"

"There's nothing wrong with me. I'm like any other kid except I have this gift."

Behind me someone clapped, slow and steady. I turned to see Shade—the translucent dark green version—leaning against the window where he must have been all along, hidden against the backdrop of the sea.

Zoe pulled herself from Pa's grasp and ran to stand next to me. She faced the settlers. "I have a Dark Gift, too!" she said. "I can electrocute people." She pointed proudly at Shade. "I shocked him."

Hewitt slunk forward, looking reluctant, but he took a place next to Zoe. "I have one, too."

Lars frowned. "What?"

"I'm a genius," Hewitt mumbled.

His pa snorted.

"I didn't say I was mature," Hewitt said defensively. "But I don't have to think to calculate."

"That makes you a numbers whiz, honey," Shurl said soothingly. "Lots of people have that gift."

"Can lots of people tell you the atmospheric pressure of any room in this building just by walking into it?" Hewitt asked. "Or the exact temperature of seawater by dipping in one toe?"

Our parents shifted. Their expressions were of shock, grief, and worst of all, regret.

"We have to get them away from the water pressure," Ma said suddenly.

"If we move Topside now," Shurl said, turning to Lars, "while he's still young—"

"His gift will go away?" Shade mocked. "I lived Topside for a year after Seablite and I'm not *fixed*."

"That doesn't mean we shouldn't move Topside!" Hewitt scampered over to his parents. "It's worth a try."

"I'm not leaving the ocean," I said firmly. "I'm fine."

"You don't know that for a fact." Ma's expression was fierce.

"I know it for a fact." Shade sauntered forward. "We're healthier than you 'normal' folk. Our immune systems are better. But don't believe me, ask Doc. There's not an inch of me he didn't test."

We turned to one another and saw that Doc was not among us, then looked up to see him standing in front of the elevator as the doors opened.

"Stop him," yelled Lars.

Gemma was the only one who hadn't left the catwalk after my big announcement. As the others pounded up the first stairladder, she finished scaling the second one and ran for the third. From the Saloon floor, I watched Doc disappear into the elevator.

"Girl, push the button," Raj bellowed. "Don't let him get away."

Scrambling onto the top catwalk, Gemma paused for a split second to look down. I knew how she felt about heights, and yet her fear didn't stop her. The whole structure of catwalks swayed as she ran for the elevator and I nearly cheered out loud.

Hand outstretched, she flung herself toward the call button, but Doc stepped out long enough to seize her by the wrist and drag her into the elevator with him.

"No!" I shouted but the doors slid shut with Gemma trapped inside.

The others continued their ascent but I didn't join them. They'd have to wait for the elevator to return before they could take it down to the Access Deck. And I was sure that's where Doc was headed—to escape in a sub. I felt Shade's gaze on me.

"Know a faster way?" he asked.

"Service duct." I pointed at a hatch in the center shaft.

When he bolted for the hatch and slammed the button to open it, I followed right behind.

As I climbed down the ladder inside the narrow duct, I heard him kick open the hatch at the bottom and clamber out.

A moment later, I, too, emerged on the Access Deck

and saw that someone had jammed a mantaboard between the elevator doors so that they couldn't close.

Across the wet room, Doc held a speargun while gripping Gemma's arm as if his life depended on it. "Take another step," Doc warned Shade, "and she goes in." Next to them, a minisub floated in the enormous moon pool.

"Think I won't follow you?" Shade asked softly.

"This is the last sub," Doc replied, training the speargun on him.

Circling in place, I saw that it was true. The vehicle hold was empty.

"And this is the last of the Liquigen." Doc jerked his head toward the empty slots in the wall. Shoving Gemma down the ladder onto the moon pool's submerged ledge, he took the Liquigen pack from under his arm and punctured it with the harpoon loaded in his gun. With a hiss, foam bubbled out. He flung the pack into the moon pool, where it floated, sputtering out its contents. "Before I go, let's get one thing straight," he said, glaring at Shade. "Living subsea messed up your brain, not me. I just tried to figure out why."

"Left no stone unturned," Shade agreed. "Must have really burned you up. After being so thorough, to get turned into the 'wealth's scapegoat. Called a fraud."

Ignoring him, Doc tossed aside the sub's hitching line.

"Shouldn't have written that article, Doc," Shade chided mockingly. "You know you can't buck the 'wealth."

He must have hit a raw spot because Doc shot him a hostile look. "Everything in that article was true."

"But you couldn't prove it." Shade's tattoos writhed across his back like Medusa's snakes. "Not after your evidence escaped."

"Get in." Doc shoved Gemma onto the minisub's bumper. Arms windmilling, she caught her balance, then scampered up the hull and shimmied into the open hatch.

"That why you came back to Benthic Territory? To collect new evidence?" Shade pointed at me. "Show the world you were right?"

My fingers grew numb as all the blood in my body went toward fueling my brain so that I could comprehend Shade's words. *I was the reason Doc came subsea. So he could prove his theory about Dark Gifts?* "I'm not an orphan," I sputtered. "My parents wouldn't let anyone use me like that."

"Maybe they wouldn't have had a say," Shade speculated. "How were you going to get around them, Doc? Bet you had a plan."

The numb feeling climbed my limbs and nearly stopped my heart. "Is that why you called my parents negligent today?" I demanded. "So you could take them to court and have them declared unfit?"

Doc's gaze jumped to me for only a second, but I saw a world of guilt in his glance.

Shade must have caught it, too, because he snorted with contempt. "Don't take it personally, kid. Doc's got a reputation to restore."

"Shut up," Doc snarled. Keeping the speargun trained on Shade, he leapt onto the minisub's bumper, only to have it bobble under his feet.

Through the sub's viewport, I spotted Gemma studying the control panel with a determined expression. She shoved the joystick forward and the sub took off, sinking as it went. The sudden propulsion sent Doc tumbling backward, and with a thunderous splash, he hit the water. As he floundered, the minisub banged into the far side of the moon pool and I ran the length of the room to help her. But Gemma didn't seem to need my help. She stood on her seat and hoisted herself out the hatch as seawater poured in around her, filling the cockpit.

Just as the sub sank beneath the surface, Gemma leapt from the rim of the hatch onto the submerged ledge. I got there in time to offer her a hand up to the wet room floor and then heard a splash behind me.

Turning, I saw Shade skid along the submerged ledge toward Doc, who frantically backstroked away from the ladder.

"Most of the boys can't sleep," Shade murmured as he circled to head off Doc, who was swimming for another ladder. "And when they do, they wake up screaming. Even now. Every time they shut their eyes, you're there—with your needles and scalpels . . ."

Growing desperate, Doc swung the speargun off his back. He sidestroked for the ledge again, aiming the gun with one hand. "Take the shot," Shade taunted, opening his arms wide. "Only chance you got."

Doc fired, missing Shade by inches. The outlaw didn't even flinch, just tsked over the lost opportunity. Doc's movements were slowing. Soon he'd be too cold to tread water. Leaping to my feet, I snatched a long pole from the wall and headed back to help him. But Shade, with his tattoos winding up his arms, blocked me.

"He's about to go under!"

"Really?" Despite his cool tone, there was no missing the fury in Shade's eyes. "Shame."

Doc thrashed for the floating Liquigen pack. Grabbing it, he pressed his lips to the hole in the pack's side and sucked in whatever Liquigen was left.

Behind me, boot steps rang from the ladder inside the service duct. I turned to see Pa emerge through the hatch with Ma right behind him. "Help me get Doc," I shouted. But when I swung back to the moon pool, Doc was gone. I ran to the edge and scanned the dark water but saw no trace of him.

"He'll get ten minutes off a hit of Liquigen, maybe," Shade said as though offering consolation. Gemma pressed her forehead to the window, trying to see downward.

"He can't swim to the surface from here." I followed Shade across the wet room, past the other settlers spilling out of the service duct. "He'll die!"

"You're welcome." He yanked the half-crushed manta-board from between the elevator doors and tossed it aside.

"There's no Liquigen left," Ma called from the refill station. All the slots were empty. "We can't dive for him."

Pa crossed to the window. "The Access Deck is nearly two hundred feet from the surface. He could make it if he swims hard." Pa turned to me. "Did Doc fill his lungs all the way?"

"I don't know." I didn't know if there was any Liquigen left in the pack after Doc pierced it.

"Without fins, he'd have to be one heck of a kicker to get Topside," Jibby said.

Ma shook her head sadly. "His clothes will pull him down."

"Then we dive for him," Lars said. "We try anyway."

"You think you can hold your breath long enough to find him?" Raj scoffed. "Good luck."

"It's a moot point," Pa said grimly. "We can't swim deeper without Liquigen. The pressure would kill us."

With a hand, Shade stopped the elevator from closing. "Lotta concern for the man who would've turned your kids into lab rats. Tell you what, if I see him out there, I'll haul him aboard."

Ma frowned. "So you can do something worse to him?"

"Aboard what?" Pa asked.

Shade pointed past us and we turned to see the *Specter* surfacing in the moon pool.

CHAPTER

TWENTY-EIGHT

"Sorry we're late, Shade." The outlaw with the dark hair and wide smile stepped through a hatch in the *Specter*'s side and onto its pectoral "fin"—Eel.

"Thought you'd never show." Shade strolled out of the elevator. "Five minutes earlier and you could've said good-bye to Doc."

"No!" Eel cried with disbelief, bounding onto the edge of the moon pool. More outlaws spilled out of the hatch, all not much older than me.

"Where's he now?" Pretty demanded, pushing through the others with his long braid swishing like a sun-bleached rope.

"Taking a walk on the seafloor," Shade replied.

Pa drew Zoe and me back into the fold of settlers. Weapons drawn, Raj and Jibby moved to the edge of the group. But they'd be no match in a shoot-out. The outlaws were armed and positioning themselves atop the *Specter* and along the rim of the moon pool. Pretty scowled at the dark water. "Drowning ain't enough. Not after what he did."

"And here I thought my news might improve your mood," Shade said dryly.

An outlaw sniggered, revealing a mouthful of sharpened teeth. I recognized him from the air lock in the sunken rig and wasn't surprised to see that his arm was in a sling. One look from Pretty stripped the grin from the guy's face. Guess he wasn't as scary as his teeth made him seem. Or else, under that cool surface, Pretty was even scarier.

"Eel!" Shade pointed at the viewphone on the wall. "Bust that."

Heading across the wet room, Eel passed Gemma, who was standing apart from the cluster of settlers. As he pressed his hands to the screen, he flashed her a dimpled smile. "You're Gemma. I'd know you anywhere." She ignored him. "Done," he called to Shade.

"Do the elevator, too," Shade said. "We need a head start."

Eel gave Gemma a sidelong look as if he wanted to tell her something.

"Now," Shade ordered, which sent Eel hustling to the elevator, where he placed his palm on the panel. Shade smiled at the settlers' confusion. "Electromagnetic pulse. Very handy." With a tip of his head, he sent Eel back to the sub. "The rangers should be here soon enough to let you all out," he told the settlers. He paused by Ma. "Want to keep them safe, stay in the ocean.

Move Topside and the 'wealth will find an excuse to study them."

"You're wrong," she said.

"Am I?" he asked softly. Skin whitening, he cocked his head toward her. When she stumbled back in horror, I saw that a puckered and rectangular scar marred Shade's scalp. Like someone had created a flap to access his brain. He shouted at his gang, "Am I wrong?"

In unison they lifted shirts, pulled off bandannas and hats to reveal their scars. Surgical scars. Eel's ran the length of his taut torso, sternum to navel. Pretty's wrapped around his ear and disappeared under the collar of his silky jacket.

"Let's make wake," Shade ordered, only to have Gemma step into his path.

"That's it?" she asked. "You're just going to leave?"

"Had my fill of staying in one place."

When pain flashed in her eyes, Shade's expression softened. "You'll do fine. You've got a survivor's instincts."

"I don't want to *survive*. That's all I've been doing, except when I was with you." Her voice caught. "Why can't I live—"

"No," he said coldly.

I was tempted to draw Gemma back. Shade couldn't have been more clear or more intimidating, but she stood her ground.

"Because of them?" She pointed at the milling outlaws whose expressions ranged from amused to bored. Only Eel looked on with wary concern. "You could at least ask them," she added, fidgeting under the weight of Shade's stare. "Maybe they won't mind if I—"

"I mind." He said it so harshly, she staggered back as if he'd slapped her. "Understand this, little girl. Those ugly clam-suckers, they're my family now. You're just old business I had to take care of. And did, when I sent you that money. So now"—he pointed at her—"you're going to keep away from me."

She nodded. Though she kept her eyes down, I glimpsed her stricken expression and a flash flood of anger rushed through me. Shade had just confirmed Gemma's worst thoughts about herself. That she wasn't wanted. Wasn't special.

He didn't seem to care as he turned his attention to his gang. "You looking to settle here?" he asked caustically.

At once the outlaws piled into the *Specter*, all except for Eel and Pretty, who remained on the sub's pectoral fin. Eel watched Gemma retreat to the far wall until Pretty redirected his attention with a cuff to the head. As they disappeared through the hatch, Shade headed for the moon pool without another word to Gemma. Or even a glance.

"Wait!" I said, striding after him. "I saved your life. You owe me."

He paused. "What do you want?"

"Your word that you won't raid another homestead. The Commonwealth did you an injustice, not us."

"Oh, yeah, we'll take the word of an outlaw," Raj scoffed.

I met Shade's gaze. "I'll take Richard Straid's word."

His lips twitched but he held up his right hand. "No homesteads, no settlers."

"There's something else." I crossed to Gemma, who remained stone-faced with her back pressed to the wall.

Shade put a foot on the rim of the moon pool. "My life ain't worth two favors."

"You're not doing it for me." I pulled a paper and pen from the pouch on her belt and strode to him. "You're doing it for her. Sign this." I thrust them at Shade.

He didn't move. "What is it?"

"An emancipation form. It releases her as a ward of the Commonwealth."

When Shade raised his hand, I jerked back, expecting a blow to knock me into tomorrow. Amusement glittered in his eyes and he tugged the paper from my fingers. "She going to stay with you?" he asked as he signed.

"If she wants."

I took back the form. As Shade pounced onto the *Specter*'s bumper, I checked the signature: *Richard Straid*.

Written extra large. I whirled to show Gemma but saw that she'd slipped behind a large rolling toolbox as if trying to make herself invisible.

Jibby stepped forward. "Gemma can live with me."

Shade's black eyes found him, underscored by an even blacker scowl. Jibby shuffled back into the cluster of settlers, muttering, "Just trying to be part of the solution."

Inside the plexidome, the gang of young outlaws waved, their expressions ironic, as Shade slammed the hatch shut behind him. When the *Specter* sank beneath the water, Gemma slid down the wall until she was hidden behind the toolbox.

"Now what?" Jibby asked.

"They really did shut it down," Shurl said, standing in front of the closed elevator doors. "The screen is dark and the button won't light up."

"As soon as the *Specter* clears the station," Pa said, "we get our subs and search for Doc."

"We all hitched our subs to the inner docking-ring," Lars said. "With the elevator busted, we can't get to the surface."

Ma joined Pa at the window. "Grimes said he'd send back a posse of rangers. If they get here soon . . ." Her words rolled off. She and Pa shared a grim look.

I found Gemma behind the rolling toolbox with her arms wrapped around her legs. "Are you okay?"

Her eyes pooled with tears as she shook her head. "I want to be born into a new family."

"You don't have to be born into a family to be wanted. Stay here with us."

"You admitted you have a Dark Gift. Now all the settlers will leave."

My throat tightened but I forced myself to shrug as though it didn't matter.

"There won't be any more people like you!" She said it like I was some exotic animal on the verge of extinction. "You must hate me."

That was a far cry from what I was feeling. But she didn't wait for me to reply as she went on, "Everyone here must hate me. Your parents. Zoe. Hewitt . . . Well, maybe not Hewitt."

I smiled, though she was clearly serious.

"But when Hewitt finds out how awful it is on the Topside, he'll hate me, too. And then—"

I leaned forward and brushed my lips against hers. Instantly her eyes went round with surprise, but she didn't pull away so I pressed my mouth to hers the way I'd wanted to ever since I'd found her in that derelict sub. My insides whirled like a comb jelly sending off sparks as I savored the softness of her lips. When I finally sat back on my knees, Gemma blinked.

"Thank you," she whispered.

That was not what I'd expected. I might not have much experience with girls, but I knew that "thank you" was a weird thing to say after a kiss.

"I know you did it to make me feel better," she went on. "And it worked. I do feel better. But if I weren't the only girl down here—the only girl your age—I know you'd—"

This time I put my hand over her lips to stem the tide of words. "I did it because I wanted to and this seemed like the only chance I'd get."

"The only chance?"

"Usually your mouth is moving."

She shoved me and I toppled back with a laugh.

"Next time I'll know when you're about to kiss me and I'll shut up."

"How will you know?"

"Because"—her grin was sly—"you glow."

"That so?" My eyes drifted to her lips again. "What am I thinking now?"

Her breath caught. But this time when I kissed her, she kissed back.

"The *Specter*!" Jibby shouted from across the room.

Reluctantly I stood. Gemma, however, drew her knees up as if she was going to stay behind the toolbox forever. I gave her a nudge. "Shade was awful to you so you wouldn't want to live with him."

"I know," she said in a flat voice.

"Not because he doesn't want you around." I pulled her to her feet. "He wants what's best for you."

We faced the enormous window. Outside, the *Specter* hovered like a ghost ship.

"You don't know that for sure," she muttered.

An eerie light flicked on in the *Specter*'s darkened plexidome. It was Shade, glowing like an apparition inside the sub. His eyes sought and found Gemma. For a moment, neither moved. Holding her in his gaze, Shade raised his fist, touched it to his heart, and then vanished like a doused flame.

"Yeah, I do," I said softly.

The *Specter* shot away and all that remained was its bubble trail. A loud crack broke the silence in the Access Deck.

"Did they just fire on the station?" Ma gasped.

"Look!" Jibby pointed to the window where a small harpoon trembled, embedded in the flexiglass. Around it, the window spiderwebbed with fractures.

"How could they shoot that from a sub?" Shurl cried. "It's tiny."

Hewitt ran closer. "It's on the inside!"

I choked with realization. "After Doc fell into the moon pool, he fired a speargun at Shade but missed. He must have hit the window."

"So long as the point hasn't breached the exterior scale, we're fine." Pa hauled the toolbox over to the window and climbed onto it. He peered through the fractured flexiglass to the layer of acrylic scales on the outside, then emitted a string of profanity that was about as obscene as I'd ever heard.

"It went through," Ma guessed.

Hewitt backed away from the window. "How thick is the scale?" When Pa didn't reply instantly, he cried, "How thick is the flexiglass? How deep is the point?"

"The exterior scales are four inches thick." Pa climbed off the toolbox. "The spear penetrated less than an inch."

"It won't hold," Hewitt said miserably.

"It doesn't have to hold forever." Shurl took him in her arms. "Just till the rangers—"

The three-foot scale imploded with a splintering crash. The sea roared in through the opening, blasting us in every direction.

CHAPTER

TWENTY-NINE

The sea filled the room with such force it set the Trade Station spinning on its tether lines. The water in the moon pool churned from the vibration. Above the splashing and shouts, a Klaxon horn sounded, followed by an eerily calm female voice. "Attention. Emergency. Scale 2093 has been compromised. Evacuate Lower Station immediately."

"The service tube," Ma shouted over the din. "Hurry!" Though everyone was scattered across the room, we splashed toward the tube, fighting against the spin, water up to our knees.

"We need to prop open the hatch." Pa hauled up the lid of the toolbox.

"Access Deck lockdown now commencing," said the female voice.

"Raj!" Pa threw him a crowbar. Just as he caught it, the hatch slid closed with a mechanical hiss.

"No!" Raj slammed the crowbar against the steel-plated hatch.

"Access Deck sealed," the computer announced. The

Klaxon horn wailed on in a demented rhythm as two more streams of seawater burst through new fissures.

Then suddenly the Trade Station jerked to a halt and everybody stumbled to keep their balance. The station's tether chains were all twisted up. Before I could shout a warning, the chains unwound, starting slowly then gaining speed as they whipped in the opposite direction. Ma caught Zoe as she tumbled past and hoisted her on top of a long row of metal cabinets. The station moaned under the torquing pressure and the sea sloshed in at an even faster rate. All over the Access Deck, equipment shattered. Sparks flew. The walls shook.

Clinging to a pipe, Hewitt muttered numbers to himself, then cried out, "The added weight of the water will make the Surface Deck disengage in two minutes and thirteen seconds!"

Pa splashed through the water, which was now up to his waist. "There's got to be something left. Mantaboards, an aqua-jet, something!"

"There's nothing," I said. "I checked. Not even a pack of Liquigen." The lights flickered and failed. The emergency lighting struggled to kick on, causing an eerie strobe effect. For the first time, I felt a prick of panic.

"This water is freezing," Gemma said, joining Zoe on top of the row of cabinets. Everyone else clambered up, too, except for Pa, who tipped over a cabinet. I realized he was checking to see if it would retain air. But no, it sank.

"We're going to have to swim for it," Jibby said.

Hearing Gemma's gasp, I took her cold hand in mine. "We won't leave you behind."

"Are you crazy?" Raj asked Jibby. "We're over a hundred feet down. Without fins, even I couldn't get to the surface on one breath."

Ma eyed the rising water. "No one can swim that fast."

"We have to do something," Hewitt warned. "The Surface Deck is going to disengage in one hundred and seventy-three seconds. And then we drown."

Even if the others weren't paying attention to Hewitt, I listened—and had no doubt that his prediction was dead on. Sirens howled. The station rolled with the weight of the water gushing in. Emergency lights flashed. Ma and Raj were right. No one could swim fast enough to make it to the surface on just one breath.

No human anyway.

Jumping to my feet, I yelled, "Be right back." I dove into the churning water despite my parents' shouts of protest. With the icy water waking my senses, I swam down to the moon pool and out into the ocean, sending a series of clicks far and wide. Agitated clicks. A perfect imitation of a dolphin's distress cry.

And it was answered—as I knew it would be.

I shot back inside the station and surfaced with a splash. "I flagged us a ride."

"What do you—" Pa's words rolled off when a dolphin popped up next to me. More dolphins appeared, zipping across the flooded room, clicking excitedly.

Ma looked as if she didn't recognize me. "Trust me," I said.

Shaken, she nodded. Then suddenly she laughed. "Tell us what to do!" She sounded as excited as Zoe after her first whale ride.

"Just hold on tight," I said. "Who wants to go first?"

Zoe's hand shot up. "I do!"

Pa pushed her hand back down. "You'll go with me. That big one should be able to handle both of us."

Jibby volunteered to be first. When he jumped in, I guided him onto a dolphin.

"See you Topside, glow stick," he said, smiling nervously.

"You'll be fine," I assured him. "Just let this guy do all the work," I said, giving the dolphin a pat.

With his arms around its dorsal fin, Jibby inhaled deeply and the dolphin dove for the moon pool. One after another the others did the same while Hewitt counted down the seconds until the Surface Deck disengaged. "You have nineteen seconds to get out of here," he warned me just before his dolphin dove under the surface.

Gemma and I were the only ones left, along with half a dozen dolphins. As she slipped into the water, her whole body trembled. "The Topside has never looked so good, has it?" she asked through chattering teeth.

"No matter what, don't let go."

She hitched her arm around the nearest dolphin's dorsal fin. "If I'm still alive after this, promise you'll teach me to swim."

"You got it." I wanted to kiss her for luck, but my lips were numb.

"Surface Deck disengaging in five seconds," the female voice announced out of the blue.

"Thanks for the heads-up," I said, which made Gemma smile.

"Four . . . three . . ." The computer voice quivered as the lower station shuddered.

"See you on the surface." I chose the biggest dolphin left and took hold of his fin.

Gemma gave a scared little laugh and then inhaled deeply. Together our dolphins dove and exited through the moon pool. Side by side we rode upward, following the curve of the lower station until we reached the elevator cable at the top. I directed my dolphin to the outside position. The dolphins without riders shot past us, heading for the surface.

I cast out clicks as we climbed the water column. Nothing registered below us except the tremendous mass of the lower station. Clicking to the left, again I received no worrisome signal back. But when I sent clicks upward, what I saw in my mind's eye made no sense. Something clung to the elevator cable about fifty feet above us. No, not something. Someone.

Had a settler fallen off his dolphin? Before I had a chance to pull ahead to investigate, the person launched himself from the elevator cable toward us. Arms flailing, the man plunged into view, red-faced and eyes popping. Doc! A second later, he crashed into Gemma, breaking her grip on her dolphin's fin. As she slid down its back, her hands scrabbled for a hold.

My dolphin continued powering toward the surface as I reached back, futilely holding out a hand to Gemma, who was just a blur; the bubbles from her struggles blinded my sonar. All I could see were the dropping silhouettes against the massive glowing Trade Station far below.

As Gemma slid past her dolphin's pumping tail, its flukes knocked her in the gut. *Grab on!* I screamed inside my head. And she did. Wrapping both arms around the dolphin's tail, she held on tight. Doc tumbled past, swiping at her, and managed to snag her foot. He clawed his way up her leg, hand over fist. Gemma kicked and writhed, trying to free herself of his weight. Bubbles erupted from her throat. Her dolphin struggled to pump its tail, while my dolphin climbed higher and higher, leaving them far below. I tried to turn it around with a tug. I tried clicking, but he didn't slow his ascent.

Suddenly another dolphin shot past. Gemma's. Without a rider.

Twisting back, I threw out my sonar net and saw her plummeting with Doc still clinging to her. Her mouth open in a silent scream.

I let go of my dolphin and dropped toward the sinking station. But falling wouldn't take me down fast enough. Not when I was racing against Gemma and Doc's combined weight. With a somersault, I swam downward, following their bubble trail. The water was so cold my body ached. My dolphin passed me, heading downward, too. I was slower and dizzy from holding my breath for so long.

I searched the water below, throwing out a net of clicks, and sensed my dolphin struggling to push something upward. I stroked down to meet it, my ears popping. It was Gemma, rolling like a rag doll off the dolphin's nose. I reached out and caught her wrist. With my other hand, I took hold of the dolphin's fin once more.

Lungs burning, I glanced back at her as the dolphin raced upward. Her face was down but the way her other hand fluttered behind her unsettled me, so I refocused my attention on the faint traces of light in the water above. Finally, our dolphin crashed through the surface. As a wave carried us upward, a cheer broke out along the docking-ring and the settlers dissolved into whoops, handshakes, and high fives.

Too exhausted to swim, I let the dolphin pull me to the ring. Gemma didn't struggle when I twisted her onto her back. Her arms and legs swayed like seaweed in a current. Pa and Lars plunged into the water, standing waist deep on the submerged step that ran around the docking platform. Together, they hauled Gemma out of the water and onto the deck. Ma gave me a hand up while Shurl stood by with blankets from the lounge.

I collapsed next to Gemma, groaning as my broken ribs hit the hard deck. My teeth chattered and my body shook. Weirdly, she didn't seem to feel the cold at all. She didn't tremble or roll into a ball.

Pa peeled back one of her eyelids and shot a look to Ma.

"Turn her over," Ma insisted. There was a panicked note in her voice.

"The rangers are on the way," Jibby said, stepping out of the open door from the lounge. Then he saw Gemma. "No!"

I struggled to sit up, alarmed by Jibby's tone. Gemma rolled limply under Pa's hands like an octopus dumped from a bucket. Water flowed from her mouth and nose. Ma straddled her, pushing down with both hands in the middle of Gemma's back. Seawater gushed from her slack lips. Ma pushed again and again until the flow stopped, then Pa turned Gemma over once more. Her skin was waxy white, her chest still. The two of them set to work, Pa pumping her chest, Ma blowing air into her mouth. With a sob, Shurl turned away, dragging Hewitt with her.

How long had she been down? Five minutes? More? I didn't know. Suddenly my parents sat back. Giving up! I rolled onto my knees next to Gemma and put my mouth to hers. Her lips were cold and loose under mine. I blew as hard as I could into her lungs, trying to fill every nook with air. Quickly I leaned over and pressed my palms to her chest, counting the way I'd been taught.

Ma whispered, "Ty."

Ignoring her, I breathed into Gemma's mouth again. Pumped her chest again. "Come on!" I shouted. But she didn't move.

I blew into her mouth until I was light-headed. When I put my palms on her chest again, Pa put his hands over mine. She was gone. I'd taken too long to find her. I yanked my hands from his and sat back on my heels. Ma closed Gemma's mouth and stroked her wet hair off her cheek.

But Gemma was tough. Hadn't she said so every chance she got? I ripped open her T-shirt, exposing her bra. Her chest was cold and still. "Zoe." I beckoned her closer. "Put your hands on her."

"Ty, don't!" Ma cried.

When Zoe didn't move, I took her hands and placed them on Gemma's chest, right over her heart. "Do it," I said softly.

Tears were streaming from Zoe's eyes as she shook her head.

"Ty, don't make her!"

Ignoring Ma, I put an arm around Zoe. "I shouldn't have told you to hide it. It's your gift."

"I hurt people," she whispered. "You almost died."

"You can't hurt her, Zoe. But maybe you can help." I stepped away while checking that no one was standing in the puddle around Gemma.

Frowning, Zoe put her hands on Gemma's chest. Without warning, her torso jumped. As my parents and the other settlers gasped, Gemma's body relaxed. Lifeless.

"Try it again," I urged.

Again, her torso jumped. And again her chest fell, inert. A hush fell over the group. Stricken, Zoe looked up at me.

"That's enough," Pa said firmly.

"It's over, Ty," Shurl said gently, putting a hand on my shoulder.

Shrugging away from her, I hunkered next to Zoe and repositioned her palms on Gemma's chest. I whirled to the others. "Is that right?"

Ma floundered. "Yes. It looks right. Ty, this isn't—"

I scrambled back. "Again, Zoe!" Sobbing softly, Zoe shocked her again. Nothing.

"No more," Pa said, stepping between us. "She's gone."

I turned to argue, to explain that Gemma was tough, but the words curled up in my throat. Struggling to my feet, I saw Hewitt gape at something behind me. I whirled but Gemma was still laid out on the deck, looking as lifeless as before. And then I saw it . . . her hand twitched.

"Warm her up," Ma cried as she dropped to her knees next to Zoe.

Shurl pushed past Pa and took the other side, rubbing Gemma's limbs to get her blood flowing. "Blankets!" she shouted. Instantly, everyone whipped the blankets from their own shoulders and bundled them around Gemma.

Kneeling by her head, I put my lips to hers and blew until my lungs were dry. I pulled back to catch my breath and Gemma coughed, weakly at first. Then suddenly she came choking and crying back to life.

Screams and cheers erupted around us. Zoe fell back with a smile as wide as an ocean trench.

Color ebbed into Gemma's cheeks as she lay there, eyes closed, panting weakly. With a trembling hand, I pushed her wet bangs out of her eyes. Her lids fluttered open. More cheering broke out. She blinked at the bunch of us, all crying and grinning like crazy people. As she struggled to rise, the group rang out with cries of "No!" "Stay down!" "Don't move!"

She got as far as her elbows and saw that her shirt was open. Next to her, Zoe looked more like an angel than ever with her skin shimmering in the last wink of moonlight. Gemma cleared her throat, coughed once more, and stared hard at Zoe. "Did you shock me?" Her voice was a croak.

Zoe nodded, beaming.

"Don't ever do it again," she commanded, making everyone laugh.

"Ty told me to," Zoe said and Gemma followed her look.

"You're right," I whispered because my throat was tight with unshed tears. I leaned in so that my lips brushed her ear. "You *are* tough."

She started to smile but then gasped as she looked past me. "It's morning." On the horizon the first rays of dawn streaked across the sky and ocean. She struggled to sit up. "The rangers are coming to take me to a reformatory."

"They can't." I pulled the emancipation form from the pouch on my belt and showed it to her. "You're not a ward of the Commonwealth anymore. Shade signed it."

"We didn't exactly capture him, did we?" Shurl sat back on her knees. "Or any of them. What're we going to tell Representative Tupper?"

"Tupper is our problem, not the Seablite Gang," I said angrily.

"True enough," Lars said, "but the 'wealth will keep laying the pressure on us. Whatever the reason, the government wants those boys brought in."

I glanced at the paper in my hands and an idea took shape in my mind. "We need one of these." I held up the form. "We need to give Representative Tupper an emancipation form on behalf of Benthic Territory."

Shurl shook her head. "We're too dependent for that."

"No," I argued. "The 'wealth is dependent on us. They'd suffer a food shortage if we stopped paying our taxes in crops and fish."

Ma caught my enthusiasm. "If the government gave us a fair price for our crops, we wouldn't need subsidies. We could afford to buy our supplies from the mainland."

"The government ain't going to *give* us anything," Raj scoffed.

"Look," Jibby shouted. "The rangers." Two wingships crested the horizon. With their spun aluminum sails catching the light from the rising sun, they skimmed over the waves.

I faced the group. "That's the point. We don't ask. We tell them that we're self-governing from here on out."

Pa smiled. "You sure you're talking about Benthic Territory?"

EPILOGUE

In the murky water by Coldsleep Canyon, I watched Gemma inch to the edge of the cliff. There was still no sign of the old East Coast. It was down there somewhere, deep in the darkness, and someday I'd discover it. Now that my parents trusted me to go where I pleased.

Without warning, Gemma flung her hand toward me. As I closed my fingers around hers and stepped forward, I felt what she'd felt: a geyser of frigid water surging out of the gorge. Under our feet, the ooze rippled like a startled skate. We leapt back from the cliff. By the time we touched down, the seafloor was motionless again. Even so, Gemma swam frantically for the Slicky. I followed, surprised at her speed. Our lessons in the moon pool were paying off.

"You said we'd see something wonderful down here," she sputtered as soon as she'd wiggled into the minisub and caught her breath. "You didn't say anything about earthquakes!"

"That wasn't a quake." I reached past her to stow my helmet. "That was a tremor."

“If I have a nightmare about falling tonight”—she dumped her helmet into my hands—“I’m putting one of Zoe’s pets in your bed.”

“Falling isn’t always a bad thing. Sometimes it’s fun.”

“If you’re demented.”

“Behind Hewitt’s homestead, the continental slope isn’t a slope. It’s a sheer drop to the abyssal plain. It’s an amazing fall.”

Gemma’s eyes widened with horror. “I’m never doing that.”

“You said you’d never stand at the edge of the canyon,” I pointed out.

“You conned me into . . . Oh, Ty,” she said, turning my name into a sigh that sent prickles down my spine.

Her eyes were focused on the viewport behind me. No doubt some glowing creature had finally made an appearance. I didn’t turn to see it; I was more interested in watching her. Her lips parted with wonder, reminding me that I hadn’t kissed her in weeks, not since Benthic Territory had petitioned for statehood. I hadn’t even tried. It didn’t feel right since she was living with us now. But that didn’t mean I’d stopped thinking about it. Maybe when she was more settled, she’d give me a sign that it was okay. Right now I was just happy to share the ocean with her.

“Ty, turn around,” she insisted.

Twisting on the padded bench, I saw what looked like fireworks in a starry sky. Balls of red light dangled from the jaws of viperfish; jellyfish shimmered like pink clouds; and gulper eels, with their neon spots, streaked past like comets.

The earthquake must have disturbed all the creatures that lived in the gorge, and now they were rising out of it, flashing and sparkling in the darkness. Each and every one, a gem o' the ocean.

The aquatic adventure continues in . . .

Coming soon!

At fifty feet down, small objects glided by—a headless doll, plastic bags, soda cans, and fishermen's nets. Though abandoned, the nets were as effective as ever at trapping creatures, and I felt a fierce twinge of sadness when we passed a tangled dolphin, long drowned. We pushed deeper, and larger items tumbled by—a TV trailing wires, a mannequin, a sparkling chandelier—as if caught in a slow underwater hurricane. It seemed as if all the junk from past centuries had found its way here, to drift in an enormous circle forever.

"This is probably a stupid question," Gemma said, shifting her gaze to me, "but if we leave the wagon here, what's to stop it from floating away?"

"I'm going to hitch it onto something big."

When the gyre's rotation slowed to a standstill, I knew that we'd reached the center. Here, the debris simply turned in place.

"Now that's an anchor." Dead ahead, a fragment of an airplane pivoted on end with all the speed of a starfish. Flipping the sub into idle, I grabbed my helmet from the seat behind me.

Gemma's blue eyes widened. "You're not going out there?"

"How else am I going to hitch the wagon to that chunk of aluminum?"

"You said that sea creatures have been migrating all over the place. If this is where all the currents meet, then anything could be out there."